The Man of Fifty

The Man of Fifty

Johann Wolfgang von Goethe

Translated by Andrew Piper

ET REMOTISSIMA PROPE

Hesperus Classics

Hesperus Classics
Published by Hesperus Press Limited
4 Rickett Street, London SW6 1RU
www.hesperuspress.com

The Man of Fifty first published in German as part of
Wilhelm Meisters Wanderjahre in 1829
This translation first published by Hesperus Press Limited, 2004

Introduction and English language translation © Andrew Piper, 2004
Foreword © A.S. Byatt, 2004

Designed and typeset by Fraser Muggeridge
Printed in Italy by Graphic Studio Srl

ISBN: 1-84391-100-0

CONTENTS

FOREWORD

It is difficult for English-speakers to know how to approach Goethe. Little of his major work resembles the forms and values we are comfortable with in our own literatures. *The Man of Fifty* is a cool, almost dispassionate tale, whose tone is hard to characterise. There is a suggestion of deeper meanings beneath its urbanity, but it is hard to construe them. It is sad and comic, and like Goethe's great novel *Die Wahlverwandtschaften* [*The Elective Affinities*], it has an off-putting coldness in its moral machinery. Like that strange novel, it turns out to be unforgettable because of its economical precision. The title gives us a clue – it is the tale, not of an individual exactly, but of an example, a fable, about what it means to be a man of fifty years.

Both *Die Wahlverwandtschaften* and *The Man of Fifty* were originally designed to form part of the compendious collection of tales, aphorisms, and utopian educational projects which made up *Wilhelm Meisters Wanderjahre* [*Wilhelm Meister's Journeyman Years*], on which Goethe was working at the end of his life. The *Wanderjahre* follow the fate of Wilhelm, who in Goethe's earlier narratives, *Wilhelm Meister's Theatrical Mission* and the revised *Wilhelm Meister's Apprentice Years,* was concerned with self-discovery through the theatre, and also with the theatre as a means of moral and social cultivation. The theatre, in the world of the young hero, is the place where the bourgeois, who are normally only concerned with getting and spending, can acquire the aristocratic possibilities of 'being' and 'appearing'. (These concepts recur in the conversation between the major and his actor friend in this tale.) In the *Wanderjahre*, Wilhelm is to become not an artist but a doctor, who discovers that he has a son he did not know about. An important part of the moral structure of this work is to do with the relations between fathers and sons – of which *The Man of Fifty* is a wry example.

The *Wanderjahre* was written after, and out of, a collection of tales called *Die Unterhaltungen deutscher Ausgewanderten* [*The Conversations of German Emigrés*], in which German refugees from the Napoleonic invasion tell each other stories in the manner of Boccaccio's fugitives from the Plague. German fiction – in Goethe's time, but also for long after – consists characteristically of tales and stories, full of significance but not primarily realistic. W.G. Sebald's great modern work, *Die Ausgewanderten* [*The Emigrants*], is in fact, as English-speakers do not necessarily realise, intimately concerned, in its interlinked tales of those lost souls defeated by the Second World War, with its Goethean predecessor. The subtitle of Goethe's collection, which is important, is *Die Entsagenden*, 'The Renouncers'. Goethe's overweening Faust famously cries out against renunciation – scornfully rejecting the precept '*Entsagen sollst du, sollst entsagen*' ('Thou shalt renounce'). But the writer of these late tales is deeply committed to it.

The importance of giving things up is carried over to the *Wanderjahre*, and is also a theme ironically present in *The Man of Fifty*. Central both to the *Ausgewanderten* and to the *Wanderjahre* is Goethe's profound reflection on the nature and purpose of storytelling. Stories are connected to the theatrical ideas about being and appearing – the wisdom in a narrative, a detached bit of life, is different in kind from the wisdom in discursive or analytic philosophy. It is itself a thing, it shows being and appearing *in action*. The clergyman narrator of the exemplary tales in the *Ausgewanderten* says they show:

'the feelings by which men and women are brought together or separated, made happy or unhappy, more frequently confused than enlightened... [stories] in which every pretension is punished naturally, indeed by chance, in which purposes, desires and hopes are now interrupted, delayed and brought to nothing, now unexpectedly facilitated, fulfilled and confirmed... in which chance plays with human weakness and inadequacy.'

Nicholas Boyle, in his splendid biography of Goethe, makes the point that the discrete tales are the way in which a German-speaking society, smashed by war and fragmented, tries to understand itself in pieces. Part of what is 'renounced' is the grand idea, the large picture. Another part is the Romantic ego. Goethe is not exploring his poetic Self, but the nature of life and society in exemplary instances. His voice is that of the guiding narrator, who in this tale suddenly decides to stop 'representing' his story, and simply to proceed by summarising and commenting.

The Man of Fifty moves because of its very sparseness – combined with a boldness and clarity of selected incidents that are simultaneously plainly factual and symbolic. Everyone's sexual feelings are lucidly drawn in their muddle – the young girl's passion for an older man, the older man's sense both of the age of his body, and the partial possibility of rejuvenating it with exercise (and more dubiously with cosmetics). The over-familiarity of the young couple, which precludes romance, and the romance subsequently conferred by danger. The confusion and also the exciting strangeness for the young woman of seeing the young man in his father's clothes. The economically drawn objects – the embroidered case, which Freud would have understood but which did not need Freud to make its meaning clear, the precise nature of the hunting poem which is to be enclosed in it and returned. Above all, the broken tooth, the precise moment at which it is mentioned, the very real effect it has on the tale. These things are delicately and knowingly comic, but under the comedy is a chill sense of the inexorable nature of human ageing, of the meaning of being fifty.

Goethe's own life is interesting in the context of this tale. He married his mistress, Christiane Vulpius, in 1806, after eighteen years of cohabitation – after she bravely defended his house and property against the invading French. She had borne him a son, August, in 1789, and subsequently suffered an agonising series of stillbirths. Goethe loved her, and loved his surviving son. But he fell passionately in love, more than once, with much younger women, and these loves led to new forms of poetry, and new inventiveness. At the age of seventy-three, he fell in love with the seventeen-year old Ulrike von Levetzow and gave her the newly published *Wilhelm Meisters Wanderjahre* to read. His infatuation led to his consulting a doctor as to whether marriage might be detrimental to his health, and to his asking the Grand Duke of Weimar to propose to the girl on his behalf. He was rejected, and Ulrike never married, becoming a nun and living for almost a century. The contrast between this real event and the measured distant wisdom of *The Man of Fifty* is moving partly at least because of the effect the former had on Thomas Mann, who described it as a tale of 'gruesomely comic and embarrassing situations, at which nevertheless we laugh with reverence'. Mann meant to write a novel about this episode in Goethe's life. In the end it was transmuted into *Death in Venice*, where the austere German master sinks into erotic obsession. The barber who dyes Aschenbach's hair and puts rouge on his cheeks in plague-stricken Venice is a grim descendant of the cosmetic valet in *The Man of Fifty*. Goethe's tales have links and resonances throughout German literature.

– A.S. Byatt, 2004

INTRODUCTION

'There are certain words that, like a lightning bolt, bring forth a garden of flowers within my deepest recesses, like memories fingering the strings of my soul's Aeolian harp – words like: longing, spring, love, home, Goethe.'

– Joseph von Eichendorff

Goethe has always been more myth than man. Author of *Faust* (Parts One and Two), classical dramas and musical comedies, epistolary novels and novels of coming of age, lyric poetry and cyclical poetry, scientific works that included reflections on the metamorphosis of plants and the theory of colour, Goethe wrote for so long (almost seven decades) and so much (over fourteen thousand letters) that even during his lifetime he was already considered a literary deity. Yet Goethe's monumentality only reached its true zenith with the 143-volume 'Weimar' edition of his collected works that was published at the turn of the twentieth century by a committed, if not slightly quixotic, group of German philologists.

Here we encounter a very different Goethe, a more diminutive Goethe. Instead of the 12,111 lines of *Faust* that took over fifty years to write, you are about to read a very short piece of prose fiction about a man who loses his front tooth, in other words, about a man who falls to pieces. There is elegance to this simplicity.

If nothing else, the publication of *The Man of Fifty* into English should have a corrective effect. It will perhaps displace *The Sorrows of Young Werther* as the work you reach for if you want to sample Goethe's fiction. *Werther* is the work of a young man – passionate, biting, dripping in bathos – while *The Man of Fifty*, as the title suggests, is the work of an old man – calm, contemplative, and controlled by irony. In *Werther*, letters function like diary entries, testaments to the soul's pullulations. In *The Man of Fifty* we have letters, but we are never allowed to read them. They are important information packets that travel about while remaining inaccessible. The soul has been locked up, perhaps for ever. Instead of a story about the tidal waves of sentiment that conclude in a young man's suicide, here we have a story about the trickiness of sharing, the complexity of claiming a story as truly your own. The slim volume of *The Man of Fifty* is the perfect counterweight to the ponderous bulk of the collected works perched imperiously on any library's or scholar's bookshelves.

Goethe began writing *The Man of Fifty* in 1807, just prior to turning fifty. It was a period in his life when he remarked, 'I have become historical to myself.' Good friends were beginning to pass away, including his confidant Friedrich von Schiller, who died in 1805, as were entire political systems that had once defined the eighteenth century: the French Revolution not only consumed the Court of Versailles, but also, in 1806, the Holy Roman Empire, that awkward political amalgam whose sheer multiplicity, ungainliness, and respect for local tradition had always both impressed and frustrated Goethe.

The Man of Fifty was not published for another decade, however, until 1818, in Johann Cotta's annual anthology, *The Pocket Book for Women*, and then in much shorter form than we know it today. It was republished in 1821 as part of Goethe's last novel, *Wilhelm Meister's Journeyman Years*, which was actually more of a novella collection than a novel. It finally appeared in a much expanded version – the version published here – as part of the rewritten

Wilhelm Meister, no longer called a novel and published as part of his last authorised collected works at the age of eighty in 1829.

In other words, work on this short piece about old age spanned the entirety of Goethe's old age. It is a narrative marked by a lack of time, told by a narrator who is always in a hurry (he loves to say, 'suffice it to say…'). *The Man of Fifty* captures that experience of death in life, the temporally and emotionally complex experience of old age for which we have surprisingly few narratives. Two hundred years ago, Goethe was asking questions about what it meant for a society to be defined by being old, a demographic truth that has become overwhelmingly real in Western nations with their teetering systems of social security. Goethe acutely sensed how the coupling of vanity and technology would have a profound impact on our social structures, our families and our affairs. The story of the major's 'rejuvenation servant' and the magical 'cosmetics case' – the temptations of perfection and perpetuity – will undoubtedly serve as a key cautionary tale as we enter the Age of Enhancement.

There is another important concern of this novella, one that is not as readily apparent from the title. In many of the works that Goethe himself translated, the hero was very often a fool. That Goethe equated translating with being foolish is a powerful warning to anyone daring to translate him. But Goethe also said that every translator was a 'prophet within his own people'. There was a certain wisdom to the fool's – and the translator's – rhetoric, to his outsider status and the nonsense that he sometimes spoke. If Goethe wrote the first version of *The Man of Fifty* at a time when things were passing away in his life, he was writing the revised version at a time when he was intensely interested in the idea of *Weltliteratur* ('world literature'). It was a time when he was reading the Paris import, *Le Globe*, every day and thinking about the *commerce intellectuel* that the dramatic expansion of print was making possible. *The Man of Fifty* is thus also crucially concerned with both the heroism and the perils of translation, with what happens when you imagine writing as fundamentally an act of exchange.

The novella opens, not surprisingly then, with a crisis of owning property. How will the family consolidate their inheritance if the two cousins – the major's son and his sister's daughter – do not marry? That there was already something illicit in this hoped-for union is not lost on Goethe, nor on the characters themselves, and it is replaced by another possible transgression – the niece, Hilarie, will marry her uncle, the major, and the land will be theirs. Possession, in *The Man of Fifty*, is always configured as something slightly perverse.

Just as there is a crisis of 'property', so too of one's 'properties'. Goethe plays with the connections between *das Äußere*, one's exterior, and *die Äußerung*, one's speech, to build a felicitous bridge between the concerns of the first half of the novella and those of the second. The major's obsession with his *dress* will later become an obsession with his modes of *address*. We repeatedly encounter him struggling to paraphrase, translate or compliment himself out of various uncomfortable social circumstances. The crisis of being oneself in the novella is refigured as a crisis of speaking for oneself. 'Sharing,' warns the major's cosmetic master, 'is more difficult than you think.'

Sharing is thus the problem and the promise of *The Man of Fifty*. Sharing means both to impart something and to divide it in parts. It means that we are never alone and nothing is ever wholly our own. As a novella of shares and sharing, *The Man of Fifty* speaks to the conditions of our increasingly media-dense social geographies today, just as it was meant to address the rising tide of books upon books that shaped Goethe's own world.

The concerns with the back-and-forth, the to-and-fro of this new landscape converge in a single key word that previous translations of *The Man of Fifty* have often treated unsystematically: 'grace' (*Anmut* or *Gnade*). Whether it is granted by the King, God, or Woman, grace is like a free gift, an act of giving that does not require a gift in return. When the widow remarks, 'Please, let's not speak of graciousness,' she is doing more than punning on the German mode of formal address, 'gracious lady'. She is telling both the major and us that we live in a world after grace, where a reply, a return, is always necessary. There are no free gifts, no first things, no original works of art. There are only replies. Thus the novella closes, inconclusively, with the words, 'Everything concludes with a grateful reply to Makarie.'

Instead of the titanic Goethe, then, here we have one interested in pieces and how they may, or may not, fit together. We have one interested in the lost and found, the incompletion and itineraries, at the heart of translation. We have one, in short, who can nourish our emerging dreams of a world literature. In what may be the most beautiful scene of this exquisite novella, we encounter the characters ice-skating after a flood has frozen over. The frozen flood allows for new patterns and new contacts to emerge, but what truly matters is that this landscape is temporary and tenuous. No one knows when the thaw will come and when these new connections will be terribly interrupted. Writing, Goethe wants us to understand, is just such a chance constellation, not a pantheon of timeless and immobile monuments, but a fortunate reply to a conversation that we will only ever hear in parts.

– Andrew Piper, 2004

Note on the Text:
The edition used was J.W. Goethe, *Wilhelm Meisters Wanderjahre. Sämtliche Werke* (Frankfurt: Deutscher Klassiker Verlag, 1989).

The Man of Fifty

The major rode into the courtyard and his niece, Hilarie, was standing on the steps of the estate waiting for him. The major hardly recognised her; she had again grown taller and more beautiful. She rushed over to him, he embraced her like a father, and they hurried to greet her mother.

His sister, the baroness, welcomed him, and as Hilarie hurried off to prepare breakfast, the major joyfully exclaimed, 'This time I can be brief and report that our business is concluded. Our brother, the marshal, realises that he cannot come to terms with either tenants or stewards. He will transfer his property to us and our children while he is still alive. The yearly pension that he demands is admittedly high, but we will always be able to pay it. We will still profit handsomely for now and we secure everything for the future. The new arrangements will be in place very soon. My military discharge is imminent, and I anticipate once again an active and productive life that will bring decisive advantages to us and our children. We are watching them grow older, and it depends on us, on them, to speed their union.'

'That would all be very well,' replied the baroness, 'if I did not have to reveal a secret that I have just learnt. Hilarie's heart is spoken for. Your son has little or no hope in this matter.'

'What?' the major exclaimed. 'Is this possible? Just as we are trying to provide for them financially, infatuation plays such a prank! Tell me, dear, tell me immediately, who can have captured Hilarie's heart? Perhaps it's not so serious? Perhaps it is just a fleeting impression that we could still hope to extinguish?'

'You must first reflect a little and then guess,' the baroness replied, increasing the major's impatience. His agitation had already reached its peak when Hilarie's entrance, followed by the servants bearing breakfast, made it impossible to solve this riddle for the time being.

Suddenly the major began to see the beautiful child through different eyes. It was almost as if he were jealous of the lucky man whose image had impressed itself upon such a beautiful soul. He could not enjoy his breakfast, and he did not notice that everything was served exactly as he liked it and as he normally requested.

With the silence and stilted conversation of breakfast, even Hilarie almost entirely lost her cheerful mood. The baroness was embarrassed and led her daughter to the piano, yet her spirited and touching piece barely elicited applause from the major. He wanted the beautiful girl and the breakfast removed – the sooner, the better – and the baroness was forced to end the meal and suggest a walk in the garden to her brother.

They were hardly alone for a moment when the major urgently repeated his question. After a moment's pause, his sister replied, smiling, 'If you want to find the lucky man whom she loves, then you need not go very far. He is quite near: she loves you.'

The major stood bewildered and then exclaimed, 'It would be in very poor taste to try to convince me of something that, if true, would make me both uncomfortable and unhappy. Although I need time to recover from my initial surprise, I can already anticipate how such an unexpected event would upset our affairs. My only consolation is the conviction that infatuations of this sort are often only feigned and the cause is usually self-deception. A truly good soul can be dissuaded immediately from such a mistake either by her own reasoning or at least through the guidance of other reasonable people.'

'I do not share your opinion,' the baroness replied. 'According to all her symptoms, Hilarie is overcome by a truly sincere feeling.'

'I would not have thought that such a natural soul could be capable of something so unnatural,' replied the major.

'It's not so unnatural,' said his sister. 'I remember that as a young woman I loved a man who was even older than you. You are fifty – even if other, more lively nations age more quickly, it is not that old for a German.'

'How do you propose confirming your suspicion?' asked the major.

'It's not a suspicion, it's a certainty. You'll learn the details by and by.'

Hilarie appeared and, against his will, the major felt different. Her presence appeared more precious to him than before, her conduct more charming. He began to believe his sister's words. He found the feeling extremely pleasant, although he wanted at first neither to confess it nor permit it. Hilarie was indeed captivating, combining a tender shyness towards a lover with an undisguised ease towards an uncle, for she truly loved him with all her soul. The splendours of spring were on display in the garden, and the major, surrounded by so many aged trees in leaf, began to believe in the return of his own spring. Who would not have been seduced by this idea in the presence of such a beautiful young woman!

And so they passed the day together. All the household routines were undertaken with the greatest intimacy and ease. In the evening after dinner, Hilarie played the piano once again, but the major listened with a different ear from earlier in the day. The melodies blended together, one song followed another, and even midnight could scarcely disperse the small party.

When the major returned to his room, he found everything organised for his comfort. Even certain engravings he enjoyed looking at had been brought there from other rooms. Noticing this, he realised that every last detail had been arranged to indulge and flatter him.

That night he only needed a few hours of sleep. His spirits were excited earlier than usual, but he soon realised that any new order often produces a certain amount of inconvenience. It had been many years since the major had spoken an angry word to his groom, who also acted as his servant and valet, because everything normally followed its accustomed course according to the strictest order: his horses were cared for and his clothes cleaned at the appropriate hour; but now the master had risen early, and nothing was quite right.

Then something else happened, which only increased the major's impatience and foul mood. Previously he had been perfectly happy with both his person and his servant; now, standing before the mirror, he did not like what he saw. He was no longer able to ignore the grey hairs, and even a few wrinkles suddenly seemed to have appeared. He brushed and powdered more than usual, but in the end he had to leave things as they were. Even the cleanliness of his clothes was no longer satisfactory, as he suddenly noticed lint on his coat and dust on his boots. The old servant was speechless, astonished to see such a changed master standing before him.

Regardless of these obstacles, the major appeared in the garden at the appropriate hour. Hilarie, whom he had hoped to see, was there. She offered him a bouquet of cut flowers, but he did not have the courage to kiss her and embrace her as he normally did. He experienced the most delightful embarrassment in the world and surrendered himself to his feelings without thinking where they might lead.

The baroness soon appeared, and handing her brother a letter that a messenger had just brought, she exclaimed, 'You'll never guess who is coming to visit.'

'Then tell us quickly!' responded the major, who soon learnt that an old friend from the theatre was travelling past the estate and was thinking of calling in briefly. 'I am curious to see him again,' said the major. 'He is no longer a young man, and yet I hear that he still plays youthful roles.'

'He must be ten years older than you,' replied the baroness.

'Indeed,' responded the major, 'if I remember rightly.'

It was not long before a cheerful, well-built, and attractive man appeared. There was a moment of hesitation as the two friends saw each other once more, but they soon recognised each other. Reminiscences of every kind enlivened their conversation, and these quickly gave way to stories, questions, and various accounts of their lives. They learnt about each other's affairs and soon felt as though they had never been apart.

Secret reports tell us that in earlier years the visitor, as an attractive and charming young man, had the fortune, or misfortune, to attract a beautiful woman; that he faced great danger because of this; and that the major rescued him at the very moment when he was threatened by the most desperate of fates. He was eternally grateful to both brother and sister, for she had assisted him through a timely warning.

The two men were left alone before dinner. The major observed, not without admiration – indeed with a certain astonishment – the outer appearance of his old friend in both its entirety and its detail. He seemed not to have changed at all, and it was no surprise that he could still play the youthful lover on the stage.

'You look at me more intently than is appropriate,' the friend finally said to the major. 'I am afraid that you find the difference with the past all too great.'

'Not at all,' replied the major. 'Rather, I am amazed to find your appearance fresher and younger than my own, since I know that you were already a mature man when, with the boldness of impetuous youth, I came to your aid in a certain compromising situation.'

'It's your own fault,' replied the friend. 'It is the fault of everyone like you. Even if you are not to be scolded, you are to be blamed. You only think of what is necessary. You want to *be* and not *appear*. That is fine as long as you are something. But when being begins to bid farewell along with appearance – which is even more fleeting than being – only then do you realise that you should not have completely neglected the outside in favour of the inside.'

'You are right,' said the major, and was hardly able to contain a sigh.

'Perhaps not entirely,' responded the aged youth. 'It would be unacceptable in my craft if I did not attend to my appearance as long as I possibly could. But people like you have reasons to concern themselves with other things that are more meaningful and lasting.'

'Yet there are occasions,' said the major, 'when one feels fresh on the inside and would like to refresh the outside.'

Because the visitor could not suspect the true state of the major's mood, he understood this expression to be a reference to the soldier's life and began to ramble on in this vein: how much military life depends on appearances and how the officer, who must attend so diligently to his uniform, might also give a certain amount of attention to his skin and hair.

'For example, it is irresponsible,' he continued, 'that your temples are already grey, that here and there your wrinkles are beginning to join up and that the crown of your head is threatening to grow bald. Look at me, an old man! Look how I've preserved myself! And all this is accomplished without witchcraft and takes less exertion and care than the daily injuries or boredoms one inflicts upon oneself.'

The major found so much to his liking in this chance conversation that he did not wish to interrupt it. Nonetheless, he proceeded tactfully and, despite their long acquaintance, with caution. 'Sadly I've missed my chance!' he exclaimed, 'and it is too late to catch up. I must resign myself, and hopefully you will not think worse of me because of it.'

'Nothing has been missed!' replied the other. 'If only serious men like you were not so cold and stiff, not so quick to call those vain who take care of their appearance. You spoil your own enjoyment of being in attractive company and of being attractive yourself.'

'Even if it is not magic,' the major laughed, 'that keeps you young, it is still a secret, or perhaps the arcana so often lauded in the papers from which you know how to select the best elements.'

'Whether in jest or earnest,' replied the friend, 'you've got it. Among the many techniques that have been tried for centuries to nourish one's appearance – which we know declines much sooner than one's spirit – there are indeed invaluable medicines, both simple and complex, that friends in the theatre have passed on to me, for money or by chance. I have tested them myself and swear by them, but I have also not given up on further research. This much I can tell you, and I do not exaggerate: I carry a cosmetics case with me at any price! I would have liked to test its effects on you, if only we had a few weeks together.'

The idea that such a thing might be possible and that this possibility should chance to occur at just the right moment pleased the major so much that already he began to look younger and livelier. Cheered by the hope of bringing his face into accord with his heart, and driven by a restlessness to learn more about the new techniques, it was a completely different man who appeared at dinner that night. He responded with ease to Hilarie's graceful attentions, and looked on her with a certain optimism that had been completely lacking earlier that morning.

With numerous memories, tales, and amusing anecdotes, our theatrical friend was able to maintain, enliven and even magnify the group's cheerful mood that evening. The major was thus even more upset when he learnt that his friend intended to depart immediately after dinner to continue his journey. The major applied every means of persuasion to lengthen the stay of his friend, at least overnight, promising horses, and even a change of horses for his journey. Suffice it to say that it was vital that the rejuvenating case not leave the house until he was more intimately informed about its contents and their application.

The major was well aware that there was no time to lose. He tried to speak to his old friend alone after dinner. Since he did not have the courage to enter into the matter directly, he navigated towards it from afar by alluding to their previous conversation. He assured his friend that he would gladly care more for his appearance if only people would not call a person vain when they notice such efforts, and would not immediately withhold from him as much moral regard as they were compelled to concede sensual regard.

'Don't vex me with such statements!' replied his friend. 'Society has become accustomed to such sentiments without giving them any thought; or, to put it more severely, it is through such sentiments that people articulate their unfriendly and ill-intentioned nature. If we examine the matter more precisely, what exactly is it that people disparage as vanity? Every person should take pleasure in himself and happy are those who can. How can a person protect this pleasant feeling from being noticed? How is he supposed to hide in the very core of his being the fact that he delights in his existence? If polite society – for of this alone we must speak – were to find this reprehensible only if it became too extreme, if one man's self-delight hindered others' for themselves, then there would be nothing to argue about. Indeed, disapproval had its origins in such excess. But what is the point of such unusual and negative severity towards something that is unavoidable? Why can't people accept a form of self-expression which they occasionally permit themselves anyway and without which polite society could not even exist? After all, taking pleasure in oneself and wanting to communicate this feeling to others is what makes one pleasing. The feeling of grace makes one graceful.

'Good God, if only all people were vain, so long as they were consciously so with proper moderation, then those of us in the cultured world would be the happiest of people. Women, they say, are vain by nature; but it suits them and thus makes them even more appealing to us. How can a young man improve and shape himself if he is not vain? Even an empty and hollow soul knows how to put on an appearance. The sound man, on the other hand, will swiftly shape himself from the outside in. As for me, I have reason to consider myself the luckiest of men because my craft justifies being vain. The vainer I am, the more enjoyment I create for other people. I am praised where others are criticised, and I have, in precisely this way, the right and the good fortune to delight and amuse the public at an age where others are forced to retire from the stage or can only linger with shame.'

The major did not enjoy hearing the conclusion of these

observations. When he had used that little word, 'vanity', it was only supposed to serve as a deft transition to present his request to his friend. Now he feared seeing his goal even further removed with the continuation of the conversation and hurried instead directly to his point.

'For my part, I would not be at all disinclined,' he said, 'to pledge allegiance to your cause since you don't think it is too late and believe that I can restore what I have neglected. Share with me your tinctures, pomades and balsams and I will try them.'

'Sharing,' said the other, 'is more difficult than you think. It is not merely a matter of pouring something from my vials or leaving behind half of my case's best ingredients; the application is the most difficult part. You cannot immediately make your own what has been given to you. How this or that is appropriately made, under what conditions and in what order things are to be used, this all requires practice and reflection. Yet even this will not bear fruit if you lack an innate talent for these things.'

'It seems,' responded the major, 'that you wish to withdraw your services. You complicate matters to protect your – admittedly fabulous – assertions. You do not wish to give me occasion to test your words through actions.'

'Such playful challenges, my friend,' replied the other, 'would not move me to comply with your wishes if I did not already have such a good opinion of you. That is why I made the offer in the first place. Think about it, my friend, man desires to create disciples, to produce outside himself what he admires in himself, to let others enjoy what he enjoys, and to recognise and reproduce himself in them. Truly, if this is egotism, then it is the dearest and the most praiseworthy. It is precisely what makes us and what keeps us human. Beyond the friendship which we share, this is why I wish to make you a student of the art of rejuvenation. Yet because one wouldn't expect a master to produce a bungling apprentice, I am uncertain how to begin. As I've already said, neither materials nor instructions are adequate; the application cannot be taught in a general way. Out of affection for you and out of a desire to propagate my teachings, I am prepared for any sacrifice. I will now offer you as much as I can for the moment. I will leave my servant here, who is both a valet and a man of many talents. Although he does not know how to prepare everything and is not initiated into all the secrets of the trade, he still understands the entire business quite well. He will be of great service to you in the beginning until you are so familiar with everything that I can finally reveal the higher secrets.'

'What!' cried the major, 'you also have stages and levels to your rejuvenation arts? There are even secrets for the initiated?'

'Of course!' replied the other. 'It would be a lowly art that allows itself to be understood all at once, whose apex can be observed by the newly initiated.'

They did not hesitate long. The servant was transferred to the major, who promised to take good care of him. The baroness had to provide small kits, containers and vials, although she did not know to what end; the sharing of the case's contents followed, and they passed the time together cheerfully and wittily well into the night. With the late rising of the moon, the guest departed and promised to return in a relatively short time.

The major was quite tired and went to his room. He had awoken early, had busied himself the entire day and looked forward to being in bed soon. Only he found two servants in his room instead of one. The old groom quickly undressed the major in the usual way; but then the new servant appeared and explained that the night was the best time to apply the rejuvenation and beautification remedies as a restful night's sleep would ensure the effects were all the more reliable. The major was forced to submit while his head was rubbed with ointment, his face smeared with make-up, his eyebrows pencilled, and his lips dabbed. Various other ceremonies were required. Even the nightcap was not placed directly on his head, but instead netting was set down first, followed by a fine leather cap.

The major lay down in bed with an uncomfortable feeling, but he had little time to reflect on this sensation as he soon fell fast asleep. If we were to unlock his soul, we would say that he felt slightly mummified, somewhere between a sick person and an embalmed one. Only the sweet image of Hilarie, accompanied by the most buoyant hope, allowed him to descend into a refreshing sleep.

In the morning, the groom appeared at the normal hour. The major's dress lay in its usual orderly way on his chair, and just as he was about to rise, the new servant entered and protested animatedly against such precipitous behaviour. One must rest, the servant intoned, one must take one's time for any plan to succeed, especially if one wishes to experience the fruits of such effort and care. The major learnt that he was to rise in a short while, enjoy a small breakfast, and then take a bath that was already being prepared. The arrangements were unavoidable and a few hours were spent in this business.

The major shortened the rest period after his bath and decided to throw himself hurriedly into his clothes. After all, he was naturally expeditious and wanted to see Hilarie as soon as possible, but his new servant intervened again and explained that one must completely unlearn the desire to finish things. Everything that one does, the servant explained, must be completed slowly and tranquilly. Dressing, especially, should be experienced as a pleasant hour of solitary enjoyment.

The servant's treatment of his master was in complete accordance with his words. The major felt that he had been dressed better than ever before as he stepped in front of the mirror and observed how elegantly he had been turned out. Without so much as a question, the servant had even tailored the major's uniform in a more modern fashion, spending the whole night on this transformation. Such rapid rejuvenation lent the major a particularly cheerful air. He felt thoroughly refreshed both inside and out and hurried to greet the others with eager impatience.

He found his sister standing before the family tree, which she had had hung on the wall after a conversation the previous evening about their various relatives. Because these family members were either unmarried, in very distant places, or had simply disappeared, the siblings, or their children, could expect a rich inheritance. Brother and sister discussed this for a while without mentioning that, until now, all the family's concerns and troubles had only been connected with their children. Now, with Hilarie's infatuation, this had naturally changed, and yet neither the major nor his sister wished to think any more about that at the moment.

The baroness removed herself, and the major stood alone before the silent family tree. Hilarie approached him, and leaning childishly against him, she looked at the picture and asked whom the major had known and who might still be alive.

The major began describing the oldest members, whom he vaguely remembered from his childhood. He continued by sketching the characters of various fathers and their similarities or differences with their children. He observed that the grandfather very often reappears in the grandchild and intermittently discussed the influence of the women, who, because they married from different families, very often altered the character of the entire line. He praised the virtues of certain ancestors without hiding their faults. He was silent about those who had shamed the family. Finally, he arrived at the lowest row. There stood his brother, the marshal, himself and his sister, and underneath his son and, next to him, Hilarie.

'These two certainly look closely enough in each other's faces,' the major said, and did not elaborate what he meant.

After a pause, Hilarie replied modestly, half aloud and almost with a sigh, 'And yet no one would criticise someone who looks upwards!' At that moment she gazed up at him with a pair of eyes that expressed the entirety of her infatuation.

'Do I understand you correctly?' the major said, turning towards her.

'I cannot say anything,' replied Hilarie, smiling, 'that you do not already know.'

'You make me the happiest man under the sun!' he exclaimed and fell to her feet. 'Will you be mine?'

'Dear God, stand up! I am yours for ever.'

The baroness entered. Although not surprised, she stopped short.

'If this is misfortune,' the major said, 'dear sister! the guilt is yours; if good fortune, then we will be eternally grateful.'

The baroness had loved her brother since childhood. She favoured him over all other men, and Hilarie's infatuation, even if it did not originate there, was certainly nourished by her mother's preference. All three were united in a single love and a single contentment, and the happiest hours passed in this way. But finally they became aware of the world once more, a world which is rarely in harmony with such sentiments.

Their thoughts now turned to the son. Hilarie had been promised to him and he was well aware of this. Immediately after the conclusion of the business with the marshal, the major was supposed to visit his son at the garrison, reach an agreement with him and bring these affairs to a happy conclusion. Now, through an unexpected event, the entire situation was unsettled. The previously close relationships of the family now seemed to grow hostile, and it was difficult to anticipate what turn events would take and what mood would seize hold of these hearts.

In the meantime, the major had decided to approach his son, to whom he had already announced his visit. It was not without reluctance, without a peculiar premonition, or indeed without pain, that he left Hilarie, even if only for a short while. After much hesitation, he left his groom and horses behind and travelled with his now indispensable rejuvenation servant to the city where his son was lodged.

After such a long separation, they greeted and embraced one another with the greatest of warmth. They had much to say to each other and yet did not immediately express what was nearest their hearts. The son launched into hopes of an imminent promotion; the father explained in detail the negotiations and decisions between various family members regarding the property and individual estates.

The conversation began to falter as the son screwed up his courage and, smiling, said to his father, 'You are treating me very tenderly, dear Father, and I am grateful for it. You speak of property and estates and do not mention the conditions under which, at least partially, they should become mine. You withhold the name of Hilarie. You expect that I should say it, that I should disclose my desire to be united soon with the charming child.'

The major was greatly embarrassed by his son's words, but because it was customary for him – partly from nature and partly from old habit – to explore his negotiating partner's meaning, he remained silent and looked at his son with an ambiguous smile.

'You cannot guess, Father, what I have to say,' the lieutenant continued, 'and I wish to say it swiftly, once and for all. I can rely on your goodness, which, out of manifold consideration for me, is no doubt concerned with my true happiness. At some point it must be said and so let it be said at once: Hilarie cannot make me happy! I consider Hilarie a dear relative with whom I hope to have the friendliest of relationships for my entire life; but another woman has excited my passion and captured my desire. This infatuation is irresistible; tell me you will not make me unhappy.'

Only with great effort was the major able to conceal the joy that threatened to spread across his face, and he asked his son with gentle earnestness who this person could be, who could overwhelm him so completely.

'You have to see this creature for yourself, Father, because she is as indescribable as she is incomprehensible. I only fear that you, too, will be carried away by her, like everyone who comes near her. By God! I feel it and could see even you as a rival to your son.'

'Who is she then?' the major asked. 'If you are not capable of describing her personality, then at least tell me of her situation – this is of course easier to articulate.'

'Of course, Father!' responded the son. 'And yet the

circumstances would be different for another and would affect another differently. She is a young widow, heiress to an old, rich and recently deceased man, independent and highly deserving to be so, surrounded, loved and courted by many. Yet unless I am greatly deceived, her heart is mine.'

Set at ease because his father remained silent and expressed no sign of disapproval, the son continued his tale of the beautiful widow's conduct towards him. He praised her irresistible charm and each of her tender acts of kindness, although the father only saw in these the simple favours of a universally courted woman who prefers one among many without wholly committing herself to him. Under other circumstances, he would certainly have attempted to make a son, indeed even a friend, aware of the self-deception likely at work here. But in this case, he was so dependent on his son not deceiving himself – on the widow truly loving him and deciding as swiftly as possible in his favour – that he rejected, or perhaps did not consider, or even kept silent, such doubts.

'You place me in a great predicament,' the father began after a pause. 'The entire agreement between the remaining members of our family depends on the condition that you marry Hilarie. If she marries a stranger, then the elegant and artful consolidation of such a considerable fortune is annulled and you in particular are not terribly well provided for. There is perhaps still another way, although it might sound somewhat strange and you admittedly gain little: I must marry Hilarie despite my old age, but this could hardly give you great pleasure.'

'The greatest pleasure in the world!' the lieutenant cried out. 'Who can feel true affection, who can enjoy or hope for the happiness of love without wishing it for every friend, for everyone who is important to him! You are not old, Father, and how delightful Hilarie is! The very thought of offering her your hand testifies to a youthful heart full of new-found courage. Let us think through this inspiration, this impromptu proposition. I could be truly happy only if I knew that you were happy, truly delighted only if you were so beautifully and exceedingly well rewarded for the concern you have shown for my fate. I can now take you to my beautiful widow with confidence, trust and a truly open heart. You will approve of my sentiments because you feel them, too. You will place nothing in the way of your son's happiness because your own happiness awaits you.'

With these and other urgent words, the son allowed no further time to his father, who had hoped to intersperse their conversation with a few reservations, but hurried him directly to the beautiful widow, whom they found in a large, well-furnished house, surrounded by a circle of, if not numerous, then certainly select friends, in lively conversation. She was one of those feminine creatures who notices every man. With unbelievable skill, she made the major into the hero of the evening. The other company seemed like family, the major alone her guest. She was familiar with his story, and yet she asked questions as though she wished to learn everything for the first time, directly from him. In this way everyone at the party had to show an interest in the newcomer. Someone had to learn about his brother, another his land, and a third something else so that the major always felt like the centre of a lively conversation. He was also seated next to the beautiful woman, and her eyes and smile were directed towards him. Suffice it to say that he found himself so at ease that he almost forgot why he had come. She hardly mentioned his son, although the young man was actively participating in the conversation. As far as she was concerned, the son, like all the others, was only there for the sake of the father.

Women's needlework begun in the company of friends, and undertaken with an air of indifference, acquires an important meaning through the artist's cleverness and grace. Practised with disinterest and diligence, such activities lend a beautiful woman the appearance of complete absent-mindedness towards those around her, promoting a quiet dissatisfaction within them. Then, as when one awakens, a word or look transports the absent one back into the middle of the company and she appears as though newly welcomed. If she goes so far as to lay her work in her lap and show interest in a story or an instructive lecture (in which men so gladly indulge themselves), then she will deeply flatter the speaker whom she has favoured in this way.

Our beautiful widow was thus at work on an embroidered case that was as elegant as it was tasteful, distinguished moreover by its large format. It was presently being discussed by the widow's company – taken up by her neighbour and passed around amid the greatest praise – while the artist spoke with the major about some serious matters. An old friend of the widow's exaggeratedly praised the almost finished work, but as it came around to the major, the widow suggested that it was not worth his attention, to which he nonetheless replied appropriately that he could see that the work was praiseworthy. The widow's old friend asserted that he saw in the case a work of Penelopean delay[1].

The guests moved from room to room and fell aimlessly into company with one another. The lieutenant approached the beautiful widow and asked, 'What do you think of my father?'

She smiled and responded, 'It seems to me that you could take him as a model. Just look at how well dressed he is!

I wonder whether he does not present and conduct himself better than his dear son!' She continued to praise and flatter the father at the expense of the son, producing very mixed feelings of satisfaction and jealousy in the young man's heart.

It did not take long before the son found his father and recounted everything in great detail. The father conducted himself in an even friendlier manner towards the widow, and she began to use a livelier and more intimate tone with him. In short, one could say that when it was time to depart, the major belonged to her and her circle as much as anyone else there.

Pouring rain prevented the company from returning home in the manner in which they had arrived, and so those who had walked were divided up among the carriages and driven home. The lieutenant stayed behind, however, and allowed his father to leave without him under the pretence of an overcrowded carriage.

As the major returned home to his room, he felt truly intoxicated, uncertain about himself, like one who moves suddenly from one circumstance into another. As the ground seems to move for one who leaves a ship, and the light still shimmers in the eyes of one who suddenly enters a dark room, so the major still felt surrounded by the presence of the beautiful woman. He wished to see and hear her still, to see and hear her again. After some reflection he forgave his son; indeed, he thought him happy because he could claim to possess so much of her favour.

The major was torn from these sentiments by his son who stormed into the room with animated delight, embraced his father and exclaimed, 'I am the happiest man in the world!' After a number of similar exclamations, an explanation finally followed. The father noted that in his conversation with the beautiful woman she had not mentioned the son with so much as a single syllable.

'That is her tender, reticent, half-reticent, half-hinting manner. That is how one becomes certain of one's wishes without being able to defend completely against doubt. So she acted towards me until now, but your presence, Father, has done wonders. I freely admit that I remained behind to see her for another moment. I found her walking up and down her illuminated rooms. I know that this is her habit; when her company has left, no light may be extinguished. She strolls alone through her enchanted halls after the spirits she has conjured have been discharged. She accepted the pretext under which I returned. She spoke gracefully, but of inconsequential things. We walked up and down the length of the house through the open doors of every room. We had already reached the end numerous times, a small chamber lit only by a single, gloomy lamp. If she was beautiful when she moved beneath the chandeliers, then she was infinitely more so illuminated by the soft glow of the lamp. Once again we reached this room and stood still for a moment upon turning around. I do not know what inspired such audacity, I do not know how in the midst of this most inconsequential talk I suddenly dared to grasp her hand, to kiss that tender hand, pressing it to my heart. It was not removed. "Heavenly creature," I cried, "do not conceal yourself from me any longer. If any desire lives in this beautiful heart for the lucky man who stands before you, then do not veil it any longer; reveal it, confess it! Now is the most beautiful, the most critical moment to do so! Send me away, or take me in your arms!"

'I do not know all that I said or how I conducted myself. She did not withdraw, she did not resist, and she did not answer. I dared to take her in my arms, to ask her if she wished to be mine. I kissed her impetuously; she pushed me away. "Yes, of course, yes!" or something like that she said half aloud as though confused. I withdrew myself and cried, "I will send my father; he shall speak for me!" "Don't mention a word of this to him," she replied, as she followed me for a few steps. "Please leave. Forget what has happened." '

We will not describe here what the major was thinking. Nevertheless, he said to his son, 'What do you think is to be done now? The matter, I would think, has been sufficiently, and quite spontaneously, introduced, so that we can now proceed somewhat more formally. Perhaps it would be appropriate if I visit her tomorrow and ask for her hand for you.'

'Dear God, Father!' he exclaimed. 'That would ruin everything. Her behaviour, her mood, must not be disturbed and upset by formality. It is enough, Father, that your presence accelerated this union without your speaking a word. Yes, you are the one to whom I owe my happiness! My lover's respect for you overcame her doubts, and never would the son have experienced such a delightful moment if the father had not prepared it for him.'

They entertained themselves with a number of shared sentiments well into the night. They agreed on their plans. The major wished to pay a parting visit to the widow, if only for the sake of formality, and then pursue his union with Hilarie; the son was to promote and accelerate his case where possible.

Our major visited the beautiful widow the following morning to take his leave and, if possible, to promote his son's intentions with propriety. He found her in ornate morning attire, accompanied by an older woman who immediately welcomed him in the most well-mannered and cordial fashion. The grace of the younger woman and the decorum of the older placed the pair in the most desirable equilibrium, and their conduct towards one another seemed to suggest that they were related.

It appeared that the younger woman had assiduously completed the embroidered case familiar to us from yesterday's party. After the usual greetings and obligatory words towards a welcome visitor, the widow turned to her friend and handed her the artful work, and, as though she were resuming an interrupted conversation, she remarked, 'You see that I have indeed finished, even if it did not seem likely that I would because of certain delays and hesitations.'

'You have arrived at the perfect time, Major,' said the older woman, 'to settle our debate, or at least to vote for one party or the other. I maintain that one does not begin such a vast work without thinking of the person for whom it is being made. It cannot be completed without such an idea. Look for yourself at the artwork, for that is what I gladly call it, and tell us whether something like that can be undertaken completely without a purpose.'

Our major had to grant the work high praise. Partially braided, partially embroidered, it evoked both admiration and a desire to learn how it was made. Colourful satin predominated, but gold was not neglected; indeed, it was unclear which should be more admired, splendour or taste.

'There is admittedly some work left to do,' replied the beautiful widow as she untied the encircling ribbon and occupied herself with the inside. 'I do not wish to argue,' she continued, 'but rather to explain how I feel during such an activity. As young women, we are accustomed to work with our fingers and wander with our thoughts; both habits remain with us as we learn to complete the most difficult and most elaborate works. I will not deny that with every work of this kind I associated my thoughts with people, with circumstances, and with joy or sorrow. And so what I began became valuable to me and what I completed, one might say, became precious. Thus even the most trivial work was considered important, the simplest work acquired value, and the most difficult acquired even more, because the memories associated with it were richer and more complete. I always felt that I could offer such work to friends and lovers, to honourable and eminent people; they, too, recognised this and knew that I had handed them something truly my own. Although intricate and inexpressible, it always coalesced in the end into an agreeable gift that was delightfully accepted, like a cordial greeting.'

A response to such an amiable confession was hardly possible, yet the older woman knew to reply with polite-sounding words. The major on the other hand, accustomed his entire life to prize the graceful wisdom of Roman writers and poets and to commit to memory their luminous expressions, was reminded of a few suitable verses, but guarded himself against speaking them aloud or even mentioning them, in order not to seem a pedant. Nevertheless, so as not to appear mute and dull, he attempted an impromptu prose paraphrase, which unfortunately did not completely succeed and almost brought the conversation to a standstill.

The older woman consequently reached for a book that had been set down at the entrance of our friend, a collection of poetry which had captured the two women's attention. It provided the opportunity to speak of the art of poetry, and yet the conversation did not remain long amid generalities. The two women soon confessed that they had been informed about the major's poetic talent. The son, who did not conceal his own aspiration to the honorary title of poet, had spoken of the father's poems to the women and had even recited a few. This was done, no doubt, to flatter himself with a poetic lineage and, as is customary with young men, to fashion himself, however modestly, as a progressive youth capable of surpassing the capacities of his father. The major, however, wished to extricate himself from this conversation, preferring instead only to be considered an amateur and enthusiast. Since there were no available means for outright evasion, he began his retreat by declaring that the manner of poetry in which he was practised was subordinate, perhaps even inauthentic; he could not deny that he had made a few attempts in what one called descriptive, or in some sense, didactic poetry.

The women, especially the younger one, openly embraced this form of poetry. She remarked, 'If you want to live reasonably and peacefully, which in the end is everyone's desire and aim, what is the point of the agitated soul who arbitrarily excites us without offering anything, who unsettles us only to leave us alone? Endlessly more pleasant to me – since I would never gladly do without poetry – are those poets who transport me to a place of mirth, where I am able to recognise myself again. I prefer the poets who encourage in me a love of the simple pastoral life, who lead me through a thicketed grove into the forest, who place me unobserved atop some peak with a view to a mountain lake surrounded first by cultivated hills, then by tree-crowned Alps, and finally by rising blue mountains, to complete the satisfying image. If one can offer this in clear rhyme and rhythm, then, as I sit on my sofa, I am grateful that the poet has built an image in my imagination that I can enjoy more peacefully than if I were to see it after a tiring journey or under other unfavourable conditions.'

The major, who only saw the prevailing conversation as a means to further his own objectives, attempted to turn the topic once again towards lyric poetry, a form in which his son had indeed achieved praiseworthy results. While the women did not contradict the major outright, they did try to coax him away from the course he had suggested, especially since he seemed to allude to his son's passionate poems that were invoked, not without force and talent, to express his heart's undeniable infatuation with this incomparable woman.

'I prefer,' said the beautiful woman, 'that the songs of lovers be neither sung nor read aloud. We envy happy lovers before we are aware of it, and the sad ones bore us.'

Turning to her friend, the older woman continued the conversation, saying, 'Why are we making such digressions, losing time in such formalities towards a man whom we honour and love? Should we not confide in him that we have the pleasure of knowing in part his graceful poem where he meticulously recounts his gallant passion for the hunt? Should we not request that he now convey it in its entirety? Your son,' she continued, 'recited a few passages from memory with great animation and made us curious to learn the context.'

As the father tried to return once again to his son's talents, the women found this unacceptable and argued that this was an obvious tactic to reject the fulfilment of their wishes. He did not escape until he had unconditionally promised to send the poem. After this, the conversation took a turn that prevented him from introducing anything more in the son's favour, especially since the latter had advised him to avoid all importunity.

Now that it seemed time to depart and the major made certain movements to this effect, the beautiful widow spoke with an element of embarrassment which only made her more beautiful. As she carefully unravelled the freshly tied bow on the embroidered case, she said, 'Poets and lovers unfortunately have the same reputation: their promises are not to be much trusted. Forgive me then if I venture to question an honourable man's word and do not desire, but rather give a deposit, a penny of faith. Take this case, it is like your poem of the hunt. Many memories are bound up with it, much time passed during the work, and now it is finally finished. Treat it as a messenger to deliver your charming work to us.'

The major was deeply moved by such an unexpected offer. The elegant splendour of the gift had so little in common with the major's usual possessions, with the objects that he most often used, that, although it had just been given to him, he was unable to see it as his own. Nevertheless, he managed to collect himself, and as his memory was never wanting in inherited goods, another classical passage leapt to mind. It would have been pedantic for him to quote it, but he realised cheerfully that its artful paraphrase would allow him to offer both kind thanks and an elegant compliment on the spur of the moment. And so the scene concluded satisfactorily for the entire group.

Thus, in the end, the major found himself entwined in a pleasant relationship, though not without some difficulties. He had obligated himself to write down and send the poem, and even if the occasion seemed somehow uncomfortable, it was nonetheless fortunate to stay in contact with the young woman who, with her great merits, stood to be so closely connected to him. He departed not without a certain inner satisfaction, for how should a poet not feel encouragement when his diligent work, which has lain so long unnoticed, unexpectedly receives such attractive attention?

Immediately following his return to his quarters, the major sat down to report everything to his dear sister. It was completely natural that his representation of events was imbued with a certain exaltation, just as he had experienced it, but also intensified by the persuasions of his son who interrupted him from time to time.

The letter made a very mixed impression on the baroness. Although she was completely satisfied that her brother's relationship with Hilarie could now be both promoted and accelerated, she was still not completely pleased with the beautiful widow, although she did not know how to account for this. At this point, let us make the following remarks.

One must never confide in one woman enthusiasm for another. They know one another too well to hold such exclusive devotion in high regard. Men are like buyers in a shop to them, where the seller has the advantage of knowing his goods and can use the opportunity to show them in the best light; by contrast, the buyer always enters with an element of innocence. He needs the goods, wants them, even desires them, but he seldom understands how to observe them with the eyes of an expert. The seller knows quite well what he gives, the buyer not always what he receives. But this will never change in the life and habits of man; in fact, it is as commendable as it is necessary, because all desiring and courting, all buying and exchanging, depend on it.

As a consequence more of such feelings than of observations, it was impossible for the baroness to be completely satisfied with either the son's passion or the father's favourable account. She found herself surprised by the happy turn of events, yet she could not dismiss a certain misgiving about the double disparity in age. Hilarie was too young, it seemed to her, for the brother, the widow not young enough for the son. In the meantime, the affair had taken a turn that apparently could not be interrupted. She felt a sincere wish that everything should go well, and yet she could not contain a quiet sigh. To lighten the burden on her heart, she took up a quill and wrote to a friend who was intimately familiar with the ways of man. After recounting the events that had transpired, she continued in the following manner:

> *I am not unfamiliar with this kind of young and tempting widow. She seems to reject feminine company and only permits one woman to accompany her who does her no injury, flatters her, and artfully lends a voice to her mute qualities when they are not clearly enough exposed. Viewers of such a display must be men, thus her need for attracting them and capturing them. I have no ill thoughts towards this beautiful woman, she appears decent and cautious enough, but such covetous vanity will readily make sacrifices as circumstances require. What I find even worse is that not everything is reflected upon and premeditated; a certain cheerful naturalness guides her and protects her, and nothing is more dangerous in such a born coquette as an audacity that arises from innocence.*

The major arrived at his new property and dedicated day and night to its surveying and investigation. He had occasion to notice that the enactment and completion of a well-conceived idea is often subject to so many obstacles and so many coincidences that it often threatens to disappear entirely. Just as it seems to vanish for good, in the middle of so much confusion, success seems possible once more, when time, the best ally of an indefatigable perseverance, offers her helping hand.

Thus the pitiful sight of such beautiful, attractive, neglected, and misused property would have become an inconsolable fact for the major if the reasoned observations of some discerning economists had not allowed him to foresee that a succession of years, utilised with reason and probity, would suffice to enliven such lifelessness and set the stagnation back in motion. In the end, he would achieve his goal through order and activity.

The contented marshal soon arrived, accompanied by a rather serious-looking lawyer. The latter gave the major less cause for concern than the former, who belonged to the type of man who has no goals, or if he does, rejects the means to achieve them. Daily, and indeed hourly, contentment was his indispensable need in life. After much hesitation, it had finally become urgent to rid himself of his creditors, unburden himself of his property, set the disorder of his personal finances to rights, and enjoy a respectable, secure income without any concerns. And yet at the same time he was unwilling to dispense with any of his former habits.

In general, he agreed to everything that the brother and sister required for their complete ownership of the land, especially of the primary property, but he did not wish to relinquish completely his claims to a certain neighbouring pavilion where old friends and new acquaintances alike were invited every year to celebrate his birthday. Nor did he wish to lose the ornamental garden that connected the pavilion with the main residence. The furniture was to remain in the summer house, the engravings on the walls, and the garden's fruit was to be his. The choicest peaches and strawberries, large and delicious pears and apples were to be faithfully delivered, and in particular a certain kind of small, grey apple with which he was accustomed for many years to honour the dowager princess. Other conditions were appended, which, though of little importance, were acutely disagreeable to the landlords, tenants, stewards and gardeners.

The marshal was in the best of moods because he could not escape the idea that everything was in the end being arranged exactly as his easy and simple temperament had imagined. He made sure to provide a wonderful meal, took some necessary exercise, participating in an effortless hunt for a few hours, and recounted story after story, all with the most cheerful of expressions. He departed in much the same way: he politely thanked the major for acting in such a brotherly way, requested some money, had the available golden grey apples – which had turned out especially well this year – carefully packed up, and departed with his treasure, which he intended to present to the princess as a welcome honour in return for the use of her dower house where he was indeed graciously received.

For his part, the major remained behind with conflicting feelings. He would have been in almost complete despair due to the constraints imposed by the marshal if he was not rescued by a feeling that often invigorates an active man at the moment when he can hope to resolve entanglements and enjoy the resolution.

Luckily, the lawyer was a decent man who, because he had so much else to do, quickly concluded the matter. Just as fortunately, a servant of the marshal threw himself into the bargain and, under very reasonable conditions, offered his services. It was now possible to foresee a favourable conclusion. As agreeable as this was, with all the give and take in the matter, the honourable major realised that a good degree of untidiness was required in life to make things tidy.

During a delay in the negotiations that afforded him some free time, the major hurriedly returned to his property. Mindful of his promise to the widow, he searched through his poems which had been preserved in good order. He also came across some commonplace-books containing excerpts from readings of ancient as well as modern writers. Because of his preference for Horace and the Roman poets, most of the quotations were from this period, and it occurred to him that the passages largely alluded to the regret of lost time and to occasions and feelings that had long since passed. Instead of citing many, we will introduce only one such passage:

> *...Heu!...*
> *Quae mens est hodie, cur eadem non puero fuit?*
> *Vel cur his animis incolumes non redeunt genae!*[2]
>
> *How today impressed upon me!*
> *So pleasurable and so clear!*
> *That I was once young-blooded then*
> *So wild and gloomily restrained.*
> *And as the years do run me by,*
> *However cheerful I might be,*
> *I recall his red cheeks with a sigh,*
> *And wish them here with me.*

When our friend had found his poem of the hunt among his well-ordered papers, he was pleased by the carefully handwritten fair copy, by the way he had elegantly composed it many years ago in Roman script in large octavo format. With its impressive size, the exquisite embroidered case comfortably received his work, and rarely has an author seen himself so magnificently bound. A few lines to this effect were highly necessary, but something prosaic hardly permissible. That earlier passage from Ovid occurred to him once more, and he now felt that a poetic translation, just as before a prose translation, was the best means to extricate himself from the matter. The passage read:

> *Nec factas solum vestes spectare juvabat,*
> *Tum quoque cum fierent; tantus decor adfuit arti*[3]

And in translation:

> *I saw it once in expert hands,*
> *How fondly I recall that time!*
> *First developed, then completed,*
> *Was anything ever so fine?*
> *Though now this object I possess,*
> *Indeed to this I must confess,*
> *Today I wish it were not done,*
> *Its making was so splendid.*

Our friend was only briefly satisfied with his translation; he reprimanded himself that he had changed the beautifully inflected verb, *'cum fierent'*, into a sadly abstract gerund, and it vexed him that he was unable to improve the passage even after considerable reflection. Suddenly his preference for the ancient language came to life once more and the radiance of the German Parnassus to which he strived, even in silence, now seemed to darken.

In the end, however, when he had decided that the enthusiastic compliment was still rather good – when not compared with the original – and had come to believe it was such as a young woman would gladly receive, a second hesitation arose: since one cannot appear gallant in verse without also appearing to be in love, he was playing a rather bizarre role as the future father-in-law. Yet the worst occurred to him last of all: the Ovidian verses are spoken by Arachne, a weaver who was as talented as she was beautiful and graceful. Although it was Minerva's envy that transformed her into a spider, it was still dangerous to compare a beautiful woman, even indirectly, with a spider hovering in the middle of a spreading web.[4] One could well imagine a scholar among the widow's intellectual company who would sniff out this allusion. How our friend extricated himself from such a predicament is unknown even to us, and we must count this case among those over which the muses have been crafty enough to cast a veil. Suffice it to say that the poem of the hunt was sent, about which we nonetheless have a few words to report.

The reader is entertained by the author's unwavering fondness for the hunt and all that promotes such fondness. Also delightful is the change of seasons that summons and incites the hunter's passion. The uniqueness of the creatures that one awaits and hopes to slay; the various characters of the hunters who indulge in such pleasures and such exercise; the randomness with which they choose or wound their prey – everything, and especially the parts concerning birds, was represented in the best of moods and handled with great originality.

From the grouses' mating to the woodcock's second flight and from there to the raven's nest,[5] nothing was omitted, everything was well observed, clearly depicted, passionately pursued, and nimbly and playfully – often ironically – represented.

And yet an elegiac tone resounded throughout the poem. It was conceived more as a farewell to these pleasures of life and thus achieved a rather sentimental air of enthusiastic experience. It had a very salutary effect, and yet in the end, as with those classical maxims, one felt a certain emptiness after the enjoyment. Whether it was from the leafing through of his papers or else a momentary indisposition, the major did not feel at all cheerful. At the threshold where he now found himself, he suddenly realised with great force that the years, which at first bring one beautiful gift after another, gradually begin to take them back. A missed vacation to the baths, a summer passed without enjoyment, an absence of the usual mobility, all this caused him to notice certain physical discomforts to which he took great offence and showed more impatience than was reasonable.

Just as for women it is deeply distressing when their formerly undisputed beauty is first called into question, so for men of a certain age, even if they still retain all their vigour, the faintest feeling of insufficient energy is extremely discomforting, indeed frightening.

Another disturbing circumstance that should have unsettled the major actually helped him recover his good mood. His cosmetic servant, who had not left his side during this stay, had recently recommended a different course of treatment, which was necessitated by the major's early rising, his daily rides and strolls, the presence of a number of busy employees as well as the many idlers in the marshal's company. He spared the major all the smaller activities, which would have only mattered for the minute concerns of the theatre, but he thus insisted even more strongly on certain key points that had previously been veiled by a rather trifling hocus-pocus. Everything was intensified that concerned not only the appearance, but also the sustenance, of health. Especially important was moderation in everything and the variation of routine; after this came care for the skin and hair, eyebrows and teeth, and hands and nails, whose elegant form and appropriate length had long been cared for by the expert assistant. Moderation was urgently recommended in everything that could disrupt the major's equilibrium, at which point the instructor of beauty preservation departed, because he was, he claimed, of no more use to his master. One could also imagine that he probably longed to return to his former patron and rejoin the manifold pleasures of the theatrical life.

The major was indeed pleased to be by himself again. The reasonable man only needs to act in moderation and he will be happy. Once again he freely engaged in his usual exercise of riding and hunting and their associated activities, and in such solitary moments the figure of Hilarie would once again appear pleasantly before his eyes and he imagined himself as a bridegroom, perhaps the most graceful role permitted in life's moral circles.

A few months passed during which all the family members were separated without any news from one another. The major occupied himself in the residence with the final negotiations of certain agreements and contracts for his business. The baroness and Hilarie directed their activity towards putting together the most delightful and elegant trousseau. The son, passionately duty-bound to his beautiful lover, appeared to forget everything. Winter arrived and blanketed the country homes with unpleasant rainstorms and an early darkness.

If someone were to lose his way in the neighbourhood of the noble estate during a gloomy November evening, and see, by the weak light of a clouded moon, the fields, meadows, trees, hills and thickets lying gloomily before him, then suddenly turn a corner to find the long row of the estate's illuminated windows, he would certainly have expected to encounter a festively attired party. How surprised he would have been as he was led up the well-lit stairs by just a few servants to see only three women: the baroness, Hilarie and a chambermaid, standing amid charming furnishings in brightly lit rooms with bare walls, warm and cosy.

In case one might imagine that we have surprised the baroness on a festive occasion, we must mention that the radiant lighting was not at all extraordinary, but rather belonged to the peculiarities which she had continued from her childhood. Brought up as the daughter of a chief steward at court, she was accustomed to favour the winter over all other seasons, making the display of such majestic illumination the foundation of all her enjoyments. Although candles were never wanting, one of her oldest servants was so fond of new inventions that it would be difficult to find any new kind of lamp that he had not taken the trouble to test throughout the estate. The lighting often greatly benefited from this, but on occasion darkened corners also emerged.

Out of love, and after much consideration, the baroness had exchanged her status of lady at court for marriage to a prominent and a wealthy rural land owner. Because the rural life did not at first appeal to her, her insightful spouse had, with the approval of his neighbours and according to the laws of the state, restored the roads for many miles around so that neighbourly contact was nowhere in better condition than here. Of course the primary motivation for this commendable arrangement was to allow the baroness to travel in all directions, especially during favourable times of year. By contrast, in the winter she gladly passed her time at home with her husband as long as he was able to make night seem like day through artful lighting. After the death of her spouse, her passionate care for her daughter gave her enough occupation, the more frequent visits of her brother enough entertainment, and the accustomed brightness of the surroundings a contentment that seemed like true satisfaction.

On this day, however, the lighting was truly appropriate since in one room we find an eye-catching and brilliant display of Christmas gifts. The clever chambermaid had prevailed upon the valet to increase the lighting and had then collected and spread out what had been completed of Hilarie's trousseau. This was done with the cunning intention of revealing what was missing rather than emphasising what had already been done. Everything necessary had been found, always of the finest material and the most elegant craftsmanship. Neither was there any lack of extravagance, and yet Ananette still preferred to point out gaps where one could just as easily have seen the most beautiful connection. While the majestically displayed white fabric dazzled the eyes, and while the linen, muslin and all such fine materials (whatever their names) cast about a satisfying light, the colourful silks were still missing. Their purchase had been wisely delayed because with such changing fashions one wished to introduce only the very latest as the culmination and conclusion to it all.

After this cheerful examination, the household returned to their habitual, though diverse, evening amusements. The baroness was well aware what makes a young woman of such pleasing appearance graceful on the inside, and her presence desirable, wherever fate might lead her. She knew to introduce such varied and educational forms of entertainment into this rural area that even as a child Hilarie seemed at home everywhere. She was comfortable in all conversations, and yet always handled herself appropriately for one her age. To explain how this was possible would take us too far afield. Suffice it to say that this evening was also a model of her life hitherto. An entertaining reading, a graceful piece at the piano, a pleasant song continued through the hours. As usual, events transpired agreeably and regularly, yet now with more meaning. One had a third person in mind, a beloved and respected man, for whom one practised these and other activities as a friendly reception. A bridal feeling not only enlivened Hilarie with the sweetest sentiments, but her mother, too, with her fine understanding, took part in them. Even Ananette, who was usually only cunning and busy, was engaged in certain distant hopes, conjuring an absent friend as though he were returning or already present. In this way the sentiments of all three women, charming in their own way, were brought into accord with the surrounding brilliance, the beneficent warmth, and the cosiest of circumstances.

Vehement pounding and yelling at the outer door, an exchange of words from threatening and demanding voices, and torchlight from the courtyard interrupted the tender singing. The uproar was quieted before its cause was discovered, and yet all was not totally calm. There was noise from the stairs and a lively exchange between men approaching. The door swung open unannounced, the women were terrified. Flavio stumbled into the room in a frightful state. His appearance was in disarray, some of his hair stood bristly on end and some was limp and soaked by the rain. His clothes were torn to pieces, like someone who had stomped through thorn and thicket, and he was detestably dirty, as though he had waded through swamp and slime.

'My father!' he cried, 'where is my father!' The women stood there, stunned.

An aged huntsman, Flavio's oldest servant and dearest guardian, entered and called out to him, 'Your father is not here, calm yourself. Your aunt is here, so is his niece, look!'

'Not here! Then let me go find him. He alone must hear this, then I wish to die. Let me hide from the lights, from the day, it blinds me, it consumes me.'

The family doctor entered, grabbed his hand, carefully felt his pulse as a number of servants anxiously surrounded them.

'Why am I standing on these carpets, I am spoiling them, I am ruining them. My unhappiness trickles onto them, they are defiled by my depraved fate.'

He thrust himself towards the door, and the group took advantage of this effort to lead him away and bring him to the distant guest room where his father was accustomed to stay. Mother and daughter were numb, they had seen Orestes pursued by the Furies,[6] not ennobled by art, but in horrifying, repulsive reality. Illuminated by the brightest candlelight, the scene had appeared all the more frightening contrasted with the cosy, radiant home. Numb, the women looked at one another, and each thought she saw in the eyes of the other the horrific image that had impressed itself so deeply upon her own.

Only half aware, the baroness sent servant after servant to make enquiries. They learnt with some comfort that Flavio was being undressed, dried off and cared for, and that, in a state of semi-presence and semi-consciousness, he allowed it all to happen. Repeated enquiries were reproved with calls for patience.

Finally the alarmed women learnt that he had been bled and that all other available pacifying techniques had been applied. He had been calmed and it was hoped that he would soon sleep.

Midnight approached; the baroness wished to see him if he had fallen asleep. The doctor resisted, then acquiesced. Hilarie thrust herself in with her mother. The room was dark, only one candle glimmered behind the green shade. One saw little, one heard nothing. The mother approached the bed, Hilarie ardently seized the light and illuminated the sleeping young man. He lay turned away, but an extremely delicate ear, a full cheek, now pallid, appeared gracefully beneath locks of hair that were already beginning to curl. A resting hand and its long, strong but gentle fingers attracted her unsteady gaze. Hilarie, herself breathing lightly, thought that she heard a light breath. She approached with the candle, like Psyche in danger of disrupting such healing rest.[7] The doctor took the candle away and showed the women to their rooms.

How these good people, worthy of our sympathy, passed the hours of the night remains a secret to us. But the next morning both were extremely impatient. There was no end to their enquiries; their desire to see the suffering man was modest, yet urgent, and only around midday did the doctor permit a short visit.

The baroness entered, Flavio extended his hand. 'I beg your pardon, dear Aunt, have patience, perhaps not for long.' Hilarie entered, and he extended his hand to her, too. 'Greetings, dear Sister.' The words pierced her heart, but he did not let go. They looked at one another, the most splendid pair contrasting in the most beautiful sense. The sparkling black eyes of the young man agreed with the dark, unkempt locks of hair. By contrast, she seemed to stand there in divine calm, and yet that disturbing event was now entwined with the ominous present. The appellation of sister! – her deepest insides were in turmoil.

The baroness spoke: 'How are you, dear Nephew?'

'It is quite bearable, but I am being treated badly.'

'How so?'

'They took my blood, which was gruesome. They threw it away, which was impudent. It does not belong to me. It all, all of it, belongs to her.' With these words his face seemed to transform, but he quickly buried it in his pillow amid passionate tears.

Hilarie's countenance revealed a frightful expression to her mother. It was as if the sweet child saw the gates of hell open before her and for the first time, and for ever, saw something monstrous. Swiftly, passionately, she hurried through the great hall and threw herself onto the sofa in the furthest chamber. Her mother followed and enquired about what she feared she already knew.

Looking up with her beautiful eyes, Hilarie cried, 'The blood, the blood, it all belongs to her, all to her and she is not worth it. The unhappy man! The poor man!' With these words the bitterest flood of tears lightened her distressed heart.

Who would undertake to unveil the circumstances unfolding before us, to bring to light the inner havoc that developed for these women from this first meeting? It was no less harmful for the suffering young man, or at least that is what the doctor maintained, who came often enough to report and to comfort, but felt obliged to forbid any further contact. He encountered a willing compliance with his orders; the daughter did not dare to desire what the mother would not have permitted, and the reasonable man was obeyed. However, he brought the comforting news that Flavio had requested a writing instrument, and had indeed written down a few words, but had immediately hidden them next to him in bed. Curiosity now mingled with the former unrest and impatience. These were difficult hours. After some time, the doctor brought a small piece of paper with lines written, though in haste, in a fine, uninhibited hand. It contained the following lines:

> *A wonder is man sadly born,*
> *In wond'ring is man gone astray,*
> *Towards what dark and distant well*
> *Fumble, wayless, such uncertain feet?*
> *Then in heaven's light and deep*
> *I see, I feel, night and death and hell.*

Once again, the noble art of poetry revealed its healing powers. Related at heart to music, it heals the soul's sufferings by powerfully inciting them, evoking them, and dispelling them in a kind of dissipating pain. The doctor was convinced that the young man would soon be restored to health again.

Physically healthy, he would soon feel happy once more as long as it was possible to dispel or alleviate the passions that burdened his spirit. Hilarie decided to reply. She sat down at the piano and attempted to accompany the sufferer's lines with a melody. She was unsuccessful. Nothing sounded in her soul to accord with such profound pain, and yet as she attempted to accompany his words with music, the rhythm and rhyme of poetry slowly began to insinuate themselves into her sentiments. She answered his poem with a soothing cheerfulness by taking the time to formulate and polish the following stanza:

> *In pain so deeply gone astray,*
> *But still to youthful jests be born;*
> *Upright on swift and sturdy feet,*
> *Come under friendship's holy spell*
> *To truly feel in goodness steeped,*
> *From there will flow life's cheerful well.*

The doctor transmitted the message, and it was a success. The young man replied with moderation. Hilarie benevolently continued, and so it seemed that one had gradually reached new ground and a brighter day. Perhaps it will one day be permissible to share the entire course of this fair treatment. Suffice it to say that time passed easily with such occupations. A well-composed reunion was being prepared which the doctor decided to defer no longer than necessary.

In the meantime, the baroness had occupied herself with the ordering and arranging of her old papers, and this form of amusement, which was completely appropriate to the current circumstances, had a wonderful effect on her agitated spirit. Surveying many years of her life, she remembered difficult and threatening passions, which strengthened her courage for the present moment. She was particularly touched by the memory of a gratifying relationship with Makarie, developed under rather precarious circumstances. The baroness felt once more in her heart the magnificence of this unique woman, and immediately decided to turn to her this time as well, for to whom else should she direct her feelings and confess her fear and hope?

While clearing up, she also found, among other things, her brother's miniature portrait. She sighed, smiling at the likeness to his son. At this very moment she was surprised by Hilarie, who took hold of the picture and was also delightfully moved by the likeness.

So time passed, and Flavio finally appeared for breakfast as announced. He had obtained the approval of his doctor, who remained in his company. The two women had feared this initial appearance. But just as something amusing, even laughable, will often occur in important, indeed in terrible, moments, so too here. The son appeared dressed entirely in his father's clothes. Because nothing of his own was wearable, he had availed himself of the major's wardrobe, which the major kept at his sister's house for those pleasant hours of home and hunting life. The baroness smiled and collected herself. Hilarie was taken aback, she did not know why. Suffice it to say that she turned her face away and the young man was unable to utter a cordial word or phrase. In order to relieve the entire party of its embarrassment, the doctor began to compare the two men. The father was, according to the doctor, a little taller, and the coat was thus a little too long; the son was broader, and thus it was a bit too narrow in the shoulders. Both disproportions lent the masquerade a comical air.

Nevertheless, it was through these observations that they were able to overcome the delicacy of the moment. For Hilarie, however, the likeness of the father's youthful image with the son's vivid presence remained uncanny, indeed upsetting.

We would prefer to see the following course of events intricately described by a woman's tender hand since in our usual way we are only capable of the most general descriptions. Be that as it may, poetry's influence must now be discussed.

One could not deny that Flavio possessed a certain talent, but he was rather too reliant on a passionate, sensual occasion to produce something superior. Thus almost every poem which was dedicated to the irresistible widow seemed penetrating and praiseworthy, and now that they were enthusiastically read aloud in the presence of a charming woman, they inevitably produced no small effect.

A woman who sees another passionately loved gladly plays the role of confidante. She nurtures a secret, scarcely conscious feeling that it would not be unpleasant to see herself quietly elevated to the place of the worshipped one. Their conversation soon became increasingly meaningful. A man in love enjoys composing correspondence poems because he can be answered, however modestly, by his beautiful partner with what he desires to hear and what he can otherwise hardly expect to hear from her beautiful mouth. Such duets were read aloud by Hilarie and Flavio. Because there was only a single manuscript, which they both had to look at in order to enter at the appropriate moment, they had to grasp the small book at the same time. Sitting so closely, they found themselves shifting, little by little, closer together, body to body, hand on top of hand, with their ankles finally touching quite naturally in secret.

Yet even amid such a pleasant circumstance and its ensuing delights, Flavio felt a painful sense of unease, which he was unable to conceal. Persistently longing for the arrival of his father, he revealed that he had something essential to confide in him. With only a little reflection, it would not be difficult to guess his secret. One can imagine that the beautiful widow had decisively rejected the unhappy young man in an emotional moment that was occasioned by his importunity. His stubbornly sustained hope was presumably undone and ruined. We dare not sketch such a scene for fear that we lack the youthful ardour it requires. Suffice it to say that he was so beside himself that he abandoned his garrison without permission, and in order to find his father, he endeavoured in complete despair to reach the property of his aunt through night, storm and rain, arriving as we saw him a short while ago. Now with the return of sober thoughts, he realised the consequences of his decision, and since his father, who was his only available form of mediation, remained away for an increasing length of time, he knew neither how to compose nor rescue himself.

How surprised and moved he was therefore upon receiving a letter from his commander, whose familiar seal he opened with anxiety and hesitation. After some very kind words, the letter concluded by granting Flavio another month's leave.

As inexplicable as this favour appeared, it unburdened him from something that had begun to weigh on his heart, and was almost more distressing than his spurned love. He could now feel entirely the happiness of being so well cared for by his dear relatives. He was able to enjoy Hilarie's presence and was soon restored to his pleasant sociable state, the very manner that for a time had made him a necessity to both the beautiful widow and her circle, and had been permanently eclipsed only by a peremptory demand for her hand.

Amid such an atmosphere it was quite easy to await the father's arrival, and because of the occurrence of certain natural events, they were furthermore propelled into a life of activity. The persistent rains, which had hitherto bound them together within the estate, were coming down in great masses of water and had swelled river upon river. Dams had burst and the area beneath the estate lay like a bright lake upon which the villages, farms and large and small hilltop properties broke through like islands.

They were prepared for such rare, yet conceivable circumstances. The lady of the house gave orders and the servants carried them out. After some initial, general assistance, bread was baked, cattle were slaughtered, and fishing boats travelled about offering help and provisions to all parts of the region. Everything proceeded beautifully and in an orderly manner. Friendly gifts were happily and gratefully accepted, and in only one area was the local official not trusted. Flavio took control of the area and travelled there in a swift, well-loaded boat. The simple business, handled simply, was most successful. Our young friend, travelling still further, also fulfilled a request of Hilarie's. A woman was due to deliver a baby during those unhappy days and the beautiful child, Hilarie, had taken particular interest. Flavio found the new mother and returned home from his travels with both general appreciation and the mother's particular gratitude. There were, of course, all sorts of stories to be told. Although there were no deaths, there were numerous tales of fantastic rescues and strange, humorous, even laughable events. Many emergencies were interestingly described. Suffice it say that Hilarie suddenly experienced an irresistible desire to undertake a voyage herself, to greet the new mother, to bring her gifts, and to pass a few cheerful hours with her.

After some resistance from her mother, Hilarie's joyful wish finally prevailed, and we readily confess to being somewhat concerned at first, as we learnt about these events, that some danger might hang in the air. We thought she might run aground, the boat might tip over, or her life might be threatened, requiring a clever rescue by the young man so that their loosely established bond could be more tightly wound. But nothing of the sort happened: the journey passed without any trouble, the new mother was visited and given gifts, and the doctor's company was also not without its positive effects. When small collisions did occur or a dangerous moment seemed likely and unsettled one of the rowers, such scenes only concluded with each one teasing the other about an anxious expression, or some great embarrassment or frightened gesture. In the meantime, their mutual trust had grown considerably. The habit of seeing one another and being together under all circumstances had intensified, and the dangerous situation where kinship and infatuation seem to justify embraces and greater proximity had become increasingly precarious.

Nevertheless they were gracefully seduced down love's path. The heavens finally cleared, a powerful cold front arrived, as was usual for the season, and the waters froze before they could recede. The theatre of the world was suddenly changed before their eyes. What had been separated by the flood was now connected by a solid surface. The beautiful art invented in the North to celebrate the first, swift days of winter and to introduce new life into the frozen landscape immediately emerged as the preferred mode of commerce. The equipment room was opened, everyone searched for his own ice-skates, eager to be the first to set foot on the smooth, pristine surface, despite the risk. Among the members of the household, there were many who were well practised and could skate with great ease. They had been afforded this enjoyment almost every year on nearby lakes and canals, only now it was on an expanse that extended far into the distance.

For the first time, Flavio now felt thoroughly healthy, and Hilarie, introduced to the sport by her uncle in her earliest years, showed herself to be as charming as she was steady on the newly created surface. They moved about ever more gaily, first together, then alone, first apart, then back together. Separation and avoidance, which normally weigh so heavily on the heart, were transformed into playful transgressions, as they fled from each other only to find one another the next moment.

But amid such pleasure and enjoyment there also coursed a world of need. Certain regions were still only half supplied, and much-needed goods now flew hurriedly back and forth on well-drawn sleighs. Even more advantageous to the region, it was now possible to transport agricultural goods from farms that were too distant from the main roads to the warehouses of small towns. From there all kinds of goods could be returned. Suddenly a distressed region accustomed to the bitterest scarcity was once again free, once again provided for, and connected by a smooth expanse open to the talented and the bold.

Even amid their enjoyment, the young pair did not neglect their charitable duties. They visited the new mother and provided her with all kinds of necessities. Others were also visited: the elderly, whose health they were concerned for; ministers, with whom they were accustomed to enjoy edifying conversation and whom they found even more estimable in these trying times; and smaller landholders, who had boldly cultivated land in the valley some time ago but remained unharmed this time because they were protected by well-made dams, and after boundless anxiety, were doubly delighted by their survival. Every estate, every house, every family, every individual had a story to tell; everyone had become an important person to himself and to others, and thus one storyteller easily interrupted another. People hurried in their speech and actions, in their comings and goings, for there always remained the danger that a sudden thaw might destroy this whole wonderful world of fortuitous exchange, that homes might be threatened and guests separated from their hosts.

While everyone was hastily moving about and was occupied with such bustling concerns during the day, the evening offered the most pleasant hours of a completely different sort. For the great advantage of ice-skating above all other physical activity is that one does not overheat with exertion nor tire out with prolonged exercise. All the limbs seem to grow more flexible during ice-skating and every application of energy produces new energy, so that in the end a blissful, mobile calm comes over us in which we are tempted to sway for ever.

On this day our young pair could not leave the smooth surface. Every motion towards the well-lit estate, where a large company was already gathering, was suddenly reversed as they chose to return into the distance. Not wanting to separate for fear of losing one another, they clasped hands to be completely certain of the other's presence. The movement seemed sweetest of all when, with their arms resting on their shoulders, their delicate fingers unconsciously played with each other's locks of hair.

The full moon rose towards the glowing, starry sky and completed the magic of the setting. Once again they could see each other perfectly clearly, and they searched for a reply in the shaded eyes of the other just as before. But now things seemed different. A light appeared to shine from the depths of their eyes and allude to what their mouths wisely kept silent. They felt that they were in a splendidly pleasant situation.

The tall willows and alders along the irrigation canals had become visible, as had the low thickets on the hills and heights. The stars were blazing; the cold had increased, but they did not feel it. They skated along the glistening reflection of the moon directly towards the heavenly body. It was here that they looked up and saw the figure of a man swaying back and forth in the glimmering reflection. He seemed to be following his own shadow, and, darkened by the surrounding light, he skated towards them. Instinctively they turned away; to meet someone would have been extremely unpleasant. They avoided the steadily approaching figure; he seemed not to have noticed them and instead followed a straight course to the estate. Then he suddenly abandoned this direction and repeatedly circled around the anxious pair. With a certain presence of mind they tried to find a shadowy patch; the man approached completely illuminated by the moon. He now stood before them; it was impossible not to recognise the father.

Checking her stride, Hilarie lost her balance in surprise and fell to the ground. Flavio immediately descended to one knee and held her head in his lap. She hid her face, she did not know what had happened to her.

'I will fetch a sleigh, one is just passing down below. I hope that she has not hurt herself. I will find both of you again, here, by these three tall alders!' So the father spoke and was soon far away.

Hilarie raised herself up with the help of the young man. 'Let's get away,' she cried, 'I cannot bear this.'

She moved so briskly towards the manor house that Flavio could only reach her with some exertion. He uttered the most affectionate words.

It is impossible to depict the inner state of these three confused souls who had gone astray across the smooth surface in the moonlight. Suffice it to say that it was very late when they returned to the house, the young pair not daring to touch or even approach one another, the father with the empty sleigh driven far and wide in vain. Music and dancing were already underway, and Hilarie, under the pretence of the painful consequences of a bad fall, hid herself in her room, while Flavio gladly relinquished the arranging of pairs for dancing to some of the younger members of the party who had already usurped this role during his absence. The major did not appear in public and thought it odd, though not unexpected, to find his room apparently occupied, only with his clothes, linen and personal effects in slightly less order than usual. The baroness performed her duties with respectable urgency, but how delighted she was when all the guests were appropriately provided for and she could finally speak to her brother. It was soon done, and yet it took some time to recover from the surprise, to grasp the unexpected, to dispel the doubt, and to allay the concern. It was too soon to think of unravelling the knot, of unburdening the spirit.

From this point on in the delivery of our story, our readers will be convinced that we can no longer proceed through representation, but rather only through narration and obser-vation if we wish to penetrate and present the emotional states of our characters, on which everything now depends.

Accordingly, we will first report that the major, ever since we lost sight of him, had increasingly dedicated his time to the family's business affairs. And yet as neatly and simply as it all lay before him, he still encountered many unexpected obstacles. It was similar to the difficulty one finds, for example, in continuing a project that was once in disarray and successfully winding the many criss-crossing threads into a ball. Required to change his location numerous times to pursue his business with various individuals, his sister's letters only reached him slowly and out of order. First he learnt of the son's transgression and his sickness, then he heard of a leave of absence, which he did not understand at all. That Hilarie's affections were taking a different turn remained concealed, for how could his sister have conveyed this to him?

With the news of the flood he accelerated his trip, but he only reached the proximity of the estate and the icy fields after the frost. He procured skates, sent servants and horses to the estate via a detour, and proceeding at a brisk pace he arrived, during a night that was as clear as day, with the lighted windows already in view, to find that most unpleasant sight, whereupon he fell into the most discomforting confusion.

The transition from inner truth to outer reality is always painful in its contrast; and should not love and constancy have as much power as separation and avoidance? And yet, when one leaves another, a monstrous gap must open in the soul into which certain feelings will inevitably disappear. Indeed, madness, as long as it lasts, possesses an insurmountable truth, and only experienced, masculine spirits will be strengthened and even elevated by the recognition of error. Such a discovery allows these spirits to transcend themselves, and, transcendent, they will quickly search for a new way when the old is blocked, so that they can immediately set out once more, freshly and boldly.

The difficulties faced at such moments are innumerable; innumerable, too, are the strengths that an imaginative nature can discover within itself, and the strengths it can invoke beyond itself, when these do not suffice.

Luckily, the major was nonetheless half-consciously prepared in his heart for such an unwanted and unsought event. Ever since he had discharged his cosmetic servant, relinquishing himself again to his natural way of life and ceasing to care for his appearance, he felt slightly diminished in his physical well-being. He experienced the uncomfortable transition from first lover to tender father, and yet this latter role seemed to thrust itself more and more upon him. Concern for the fate of Hilarie and his family always occurred to him first, and only later would the feelings of love, infatuation, and a desire for greater intimacy develop. And when he imagined Hilarie in his arms, he wished more for her happiness than the pleasure of possessing her. Indeed, if he were to take pure enjoyment in the thought of her, he first had to summon up her divinely expressed infatuation, to think of that moment when she had unexpectedly devoted herself to him.

But now he had seen the young couple before him united in the clearest night, had seen his beloved collapse, her head placed gently in his lap, had seen how they both ignored his promise to return with help and did not wait for him at the appointed place, how they had disappeared into the night, leaving him alone in the gloomiest of circumstances. Who could share these feelings and not despair?

Though accustomed to being together and hoping for closer union, the family remained apart in dismay. Hilarie stubbornly kept to her room, while the major summoned his strength to learn of the earlier course of events from his son. The misfortune, he learnt, was caused by a feminine transgression on the part of the widow. In order not to lose Flavio, her passionate admirer, to another woman who had betrayed her intentions to him, the widow addressed more favour towards him than was appropriate. Excited and emboldened, he pursued his aims with intensity, almost to the point of impertinence. Thence followed first repulsion and discord, then finally a decisive break irreparably ended the entire relationship.

Nothing else remains for fatherly indulgence than to regret the errors of their children when they have unhappy outcomes and, where possible, to repair them; and if such mistakes pass more pardonably than one might have dared to hope, they are to be forgiven and forgotten. After a little consideration and discussion, Flavio travelled to the newly acquired property to care for certain affairs in place of his father. He was to remain there until the conclusion of his leave and then return to his regiment, which in the meantime had been relocated to a different garrison.

The major occupied himself for several days with the opening of letters and packages that had accumulated during his long time away. Among other things, he found a letter from his cosmetic friend, the well-preserved actor. Informed by the discharged servant of the major's circumstances and his intention to marry, the actor pleasantly discussed the causes for concern that one ought to bear in mind in such an undertaking. He handled the matter in his usual way and asked the major to remember that the best cosmetic technique for a man of a certain age was to distance himself from the fair sex and enjoy a laudable and comfortable freedom. Smiling, the major showed the paper to his sister, noting the importance of its contents in jest, but also seriously enough. In the meantime, he had composed a poem, which we are not capable of reciting in verse right now, but whose content is nonetheless distinguished through its elegant metaphors and charming turns of phrase:

> *The late moon that still shines honourably at night pales before the rising sun. Love's madness in old age disappears in the presence of passionate youth. The spruce that appears fresh and robust in winter looks brown and discoloured in the spring next to the bright green of the birch trees.*

We will credit neither philosophy nor poetry alone here as the crucial accomplice to a final resolution. Just as a small event can often have the most important consequences, so, too, can it often be decisive when wavering sentiments prevail and the scales favour one side over another. The major had recently lost a front tooth and he was afraid that he might lose the other. An artificial replacement was, to his way of thinking, out of the question, and to court a young lover with this deficiency began to seem deeply humiliating to him, especially now that he found himself under the same roof as her. Such an event might have had less of an effect had it happened earlier or later, but coming at precisely this moment, it seemed repulsive to a person accustomed to a healthy wholeness. It was as though the keystone of his organic being was missing and the remaining arch threatened to collapse, piece by piece.

Even so, the major spoke to his sister judiciously and reasonably about the matter, despite its appearing to be so confused. They had to confess that they were now approaching their goal, but via a detour. They were very close and had only been carelessly distanced from it by chance, by some external cause, by the error of an inexperienced child.

They found nothing more natural than to persevere on this path and establish a union between the children. They would dedicate all their parental attentions to this cause, faithfully and without respite, and they were certain they could secure the means to achieve this end. In complete agreement with her brother, the baroness went to Hilarie's room. She was sitting at the piano, singing to her own accompaniment, and greeting her guest with a cheerful expression and bow, she seemed to invite her to listen. It was a pleasant, comforting song, expressing a mood that greatly pleased her mother.

After she had concluded the song, Hilarie stood up and, before her cautious mother was able to begin speaking, she said, 'Dearest Mother! I am glad that we were silent for so long on this most important matter. I am grateful that you did not speak of it, but now it is time to explain ourselves, if it pleases you. What do you say?'

Delighted with the calm and gentleness of her daughter's mood, the baroness began at once a reasoned depiction of earlier times, of the personality of her brother and his servants. She acknowledged the impression that this uniquely honourable man, when a young woman had come to know him so intimately, would necessarily make on an independent heart. She acknowledged, too, that instead of a child's reverence or trust, it was no doubt quite possible to develop an infatuation that seemed like love or passion. Hilarie listened attentively, and communicated her complete agreement through affirmative gestures and signals. Her mother moved on to the son, and the young woman let her eyelashes fall. Although the speaker could not find such praiseworthy arguments for the son as she had for the father, she emphasised their similarity and the favour that this gave to the youth, who, if chosen as an appropriate marital partner for life, would promise to become more like his father over time. Here, too, Hilarie seemed to agree, although a somewhat earnest look and an occasional lowering of her eyes betrayed a certain inner emotion that was, in this case, completely natural. The conversation continued by turning towards the fortunate and, to a degree, inevitable circumstances. The decisive comparison, the excellent profit for the present, the prospects unfolding in certain directions, all this was truthfully depicted, just as certain allusions were also impossible to exclude, as Hilarie herself must surely remember that she was once engaged, even if only in jest, to the cousin with whom she had grown up. After all was said, the mother offered the self-evident conclusion that now, with her permission and that of Hilarie's uncle, the union of the young couple could occur immediately.

With a calm voice and gaze, Hilarie responded that she could not immediately agree to this conclusion, arguing quite beautifully and charmingly to the contrary what any other delicate soul would no doubt also feel here, which we will nonetheless not undertake to elaborate in words.

Reasonable people, when they have rationally imagined how to resolve some complication or achieve some goal, and have thus clarified and arranged all possible arguments, feel rather unpleasantly perplexed when precisely the person who is supposed to participate in fostering their own happiness reveals a completely different opinion and, for reasons that lie deep in the heart, opposes a course of action that is as laudable as it is necessary. Thus they conversed without convincing one another. Reason could not penetrate emotion; emotion did not wish to yield to the useful or the necessary. The conversation became heated, reason's sharp edge cut an already wounded heart that was proceeding no longer moderately, but passionately. Finally, the mother withdrew, astonished by the nobility and dignity of the young woman as she emphasised with energy and sincerity the impropriety, indeed the criminality, of such a union.

One can imagine the confused state in which the baroness returned to her brother. Perhaps one can also understand, even if incompletely, how the major, who was flattered in his heart by this decisive refusal, stood before his sister both hopeless and yet consoled. Freed from his earlier shame, the event, which had become the most delicate matter of honour, seemed to have reached an equilibrium within his heart. He concealed this feeling from his sister for the moment and hid his painful satisfaction by saying what was completely natural in this situation: that they must not hurry anything, but rather offer the good child time to choose voluntarily the newly opened path which was gradually being revealed to her.

We can hardly expect our readers to pass from these gripping inner moments to the external actions on which so much now depends. While the baroness granted her daughter the freedom to pass her days comfortably with music and song, drawing and embroidering, reading alone and aloud, the major occupied himself during the coming spring with bringing the family affairs into order. The son, who now saw himself as a future wealthy landowner and, as he could hardly doubt, as Hilarie's lucky husband, felt for the first time an aspiration to military fame and rank should the looming war commence. And so, amid this momentary calm, one felt certain that the riddle, which seemed to depend on a mere whim, would soon be clarified and resolved.

Unfortunately, there was no peace of mind to be had during the apparent repose. The baroness waited daily, but in vain, for her daughter's change of heart. Only infrequently and modestly, and yet, on important occasions, decisively, would Hilarie disclose that she remained certain of her conviction as one can only for something that has become inwardly true whether it is in accordance with the surrounding world or not. The major was divided: he would feel forever wounded if Hilarie were to choose his son, but if she were to choose him, he was equally convinced that he must refuse her hand.

We must pity a good man with such concerns, such torments hovering unceasingly before him like a coursing fog that at times highlights the realities of the day's urgent business and at times obscures all that is present. Such wavering irresolution swirled in the mind's eye of the major, and just as the challenges of the day summoned forth swift, efficient activity, it was during the hours when he lay awake at night that all these repulsive elements formed and continually reformed, dancing around in the most unpleasant circles in his mind. Such eternally recurring visions brought him to a point that we could almost call despair. Activity and productivity, normally the surest remedies against such a condition, scarcely had a palliative, let alone a gratifying effect now.

In such a state, our friend received a letter in an unknown hand inviting him to come to the post office of a nearby town where a traveller urgently wished to speak to him. Accustomed to such requests because of his business and worldly connections, the major was even less inclined to delay because the uninhibited, hurried script seemed slightly familiar to him. Calm and composed in his usual way, he travelled to the specified place where in the familiar, almost rustic parlour he was met by the beautiful widow, who was even more beautiful and graceful than when he had left her. Whether our imagination is incapable of sustaining an image of excellence and recalling it completely, or whether this emotional affair had indeed lent her even more appeal, it required twice as much composure to conceal his astonishment and his confusion beneath the appearance of the most general courtesy. He greeted her formally with an embarrassed coldness.

'Less ceremony, my friend!' she cried. 'I certainly did not call you here amongst the white walls of these ignoble surroundings just for that. Such a poor setting does not demand that we entertain ourselves in such a polite fashion. I free my heart from a heavy burden when I say, when I confess: I have caused much mischief in your home.' Startled, the major stepped back. 'I know everything,' she continued. 'There is no need for explanations. You and Hilarie, Hilarie and Flavio, your good sister, I feel pity for all of you.'

Her speech faltered, her beautiful eyelashes were unable to restrain the overflowing tears, her cheeks flushed – she was more beautiful than ever. The noble major stood before her in total confusion, pierced by an unfamiliar feeling.

'Let us sit,' said the beautiful creature, drying her eyes. 'Forgive me, feel pity for me, you see how I have been punished.' She covered her eyes once more with her embroidered handkerchief to conceal how bitterly she was crying.

'Enlighten me, gracious lady,' he said with haste.

'Please, let's not speak of graciousness,' she replied, smiling divinely. 'Call me your friend, you have no truer one. Well, my friend, I know everything. I know the situation of the entire family in every detail. I am familiar with every sentiment and sorrow.'

'How could you have learnt so much?'

'Personal confessions. This hand will not be unknown to you.' She passed him a few folded letters.

'The hand of my sister – letters, several, in that careless script, intimate ones! Were you ever in contact with her?'

'Not directly, but indirectly for some time. Here is the address: "To ***".'

'A new riddle: "To Makarie, the most discreet of all women."'

'Thus she is the confidante, the confessor of all distressed souls, of all those who have lost themselves, but who wish to find themselves once more and do not know where to look.'

'Thank God!' he cried, 'that such mediation was found. I thought it inappropriate to beseech her; bless my sister that she did. For I, too, am familiar with examples of how this exquisite woman has held up a kind of magic moral mirror to an unhappy man and revealed a pure, beautiful inner self beneath an exterior in disarray, so that he is suddenly satisfied with himself and summoned to a new life.'

'She showed this kindness to me, too,' replied the beautiful widow, and in this moment our friend decisively felt, even if it remained unclear to him, that there emerged from this remarkable person, who otherwise seemed isolated in her eccentricity, a morally beautiful, committed, and generous soul.

'I was not unhappy, merely unsettled,' she continued. 'I no longer properly belonged to myself, and in the end this meant that I was not happy. I no longer liked myself; I could rearrange myself in front of the mirror as much as I wished, it always seemed as though I was dressing for a masquerade. But ever since she placed her mirror in front of me, ever since I became aware of how one could adorn oneself from the inside out, I once again see myself as beautiful.'

She said this between smiling and crying and was, one had to admit, more than charming. She seemed worthy of esteem and worthy of an eternally faithful devotion.

'And now, my friend, let us quickly compose ourselves. Here are the letters! You will require perhaps an hour, more if you wish, to read and reread them, to reflect and prepare yourself. After that our circumstances will be decided with just a few words.'

She left him alone in order to stroll through the garden, and he unfolded the correspondence between the baroness and Makarie, whose contents we will now summarise.

The baroness complains about the beautiful widow. It is revealed how a woman perceives another and judges her severely. But the conversation is only about exteriors and expressions, it never concerns the inside.

Then a milder judgement by Makarie. The depiction of such a soul from the inside out. The exterior appears as a consequence of chance, hardly to be blamed, perhaps to be excused. Then the baroness reports the son's madness and folly, the growing attachment of the young pair, the father's arrival, Hilarie's decisive refusal. Everywhere one finds Makarie's responses to be absolutely fair. They derive from the fundamental conviction that moral improvement must proceed from this. Finally, she delivers the entire correspondence to the beautiful widow whose divine inner beauty shines through and begins to glorify her exterior. Everything concludes with a grateful reply to Makarie.[8]

NOTES

1. In Greek mythology, Penelope was the wife of Odysseus. While she waited many years for her husband to return from the Trojan War, Penelope was harassed by a large number of suitors. She put them off by stating that she would not choose a new husband until she had finished weaving a shroud for Odysseus' father, Laertes. She continued weaving by day, and by night unravelled what she has completed, thus endlessly delaying a decision.

2. 'Alas! Why, when I was a boy, did I not feel the way I do today? / Or why, feeling the way I do now, cannot I have my youthful beauty back?' (Horace, *Odes* IV.10) The lines concern what an older man would say upon looking in the mirror.

3. 'It was a pleasure, not only to see the finished products, but also to see them being made, because there was such grace in her way of working.' (Ovid, *Metamorphoses* VI.17–18)

4. In Greek mythology, Arachne was a young Lydian woman whose skill at weaving led her to challenge Athena, goddess of crafts, to a contest. Arachne's weaving was so good that Athena tore it to pieces in a jealous rage. Arachne was about to hang herself, when Athena took pity and transformed her into a spider instead.

5. The bird imagery here is drawn from the familiar symbols of the huntsman's life and refers to the changing seasons, beginning with mating in spring and ending with nesting in autumn and winter.

6. In Greek mythology, Orestes was the son of Agamemnon, King of Mycenae, and Clytemnestra. After Agamemnon's victorious return from the Trojan War, he was murdered in the bath by his wife and her lover. Orestes, in turn, killed his mother, thus incurring the terrifying wrath and relentless pursuit of the Furies, goddesses of retribution.

7. Psyche was a mortal girl, loved in secret by the Greek god of love, Eros. He visited her only by night, leaving before dawn, and warned Psyche that if she tried to discover who he was, he would leave her for ever. Eventually, persuaded by her sisters, she approached him with a lamp as he slept, in order to catch a glimpse of his face. Eros was awakened by a drop of hot oil, and abandoned her as he had threatened.

8. The ambiguous conclusion to *The Man of Fifty* is clarified towards the end of *Wilhelm Meister's Journeyman Years*, the collection in which the novella appeared. In Chapter 14 of Book III, we are told:

> 'We should not, in view of our role as narrator, allow these cherished characters, who earlier claimed so much of our interest, to slip away to such distant places without learning something more specific about their subsequent plans and activities, especially since we have heard nothing from them in such a long time. […]

'Hilarie returned with her spouse, who was now a captain and a wealthy landowner. Flavio, her husband, vigorous, cheerful and charming enough, appeared to capture her infatuation completely. It is likely that she had indeed forgiven the past; Makarie, at least, found no reason to mention it. The pair had just returned from a meaningful and well-spent trip to the South to replace the major in his house, who, with the irresistible widow who had now become his spouse, wanted to breathe in some of that paradisical air for his own refreshment.'

Johann Wolfgang von Goethe was born in Frankfurt am Main in 1749 to Johann Caspar Goethe, an Imperial Councillor, and Katherine Elizabeth Textor, the daughter of the mayor of Frankfurt. In 1765 he was sent, against his wishes, to Leipzig to study Law. An unhappy affair inspired his first play, *Caprice*, which appeared in 1767. Then followed a period of illness, during which time he published some lyric poems. He eventually completed his studies in Strasbourg in 1771, and went on to practise Law.

Goethe's first novel, *Die Leiden des jungen Werthers* [*The Sorrows of Young Werther*], was published in 1774. Partly autobiographical, it was given a sensational reception throughout Europe, and led to Goethe's recognition as a leading figure in the *Sturm und Drang* movement. The following year he was invited to the Court of the Duke of Weimar, where he remained for much of his life, occupying various government positions. In 1786 he travelled to Italy, a period of his life he later recounted in *Die italienische Reise* [*Italian Journey*] (1816–17). His stay there instilled in him a passion for the classical ideal, and a move away from his earlier *Sturm und Drang* tendencies. The works that followed – *Iphigenie auf Tauris* (1787), *Egmont* (1788), and *Torquato Tasso* (1789) among them – clearly demonstrate this new influence.

From 1796 Goethe was occupied by his Wilhelm Meister series. The first instalment, *Wilhelm Meisters Lehrjahre* [*The Apprenticeship of Wilhem Meister*] (1796), soon became the prototype for the German *Bildungsroman*. The series was completed in 1829 with *Wilhelm Meisters Wanderjahre* [*Wilhelm Meister's Journeyman Years*]. Goethe is, however, probably best remembered for his poem, *Faust*, which was based on the popular Renaissance legend of a famous German alchemist who supposedly sold his soul to the devil for insight into the secret laws of nature. The legend was first printed in 1587 as a popular chapbook entitled *Historia von D. Johann Fausten*, on which Christopher Marlowe's well-known play, *Dr Faustus*, was based. The first part of Goethe's *Faust* appeared in 1808; the second shortly after his death in 1832. He was buried in the same mausoleum as Friedrich von Schiller, who had died a quarter of a century earlier.

Andrew Piper is currently a doctoral candidate in the Department of Germanic Languages at Columbia University in New York City. He is completing his dissertation on Goethe and the rise of print culture in the early nineteenth century.

HESPERUS PRESS CLASSICS

Hesperus Press, as suggested by the Latin motto, is committed to bringing near what is far – far both in space and time. Works written by the greatest authors, and unjustly neglected or simply little known in the English-speaking world, are made accessible through new translations and a completely fresh editorial approach. Through these classic works, the reader is introduced to the greatest writers from all times and all cultures.

For more information on Hesperus Press, please visit our website: **www.hesperuspress.com**

ET REMOTISSIMA PROPE

SELECTED TITLES FROM HESPERUS PRESS